THE EYE OF THE BEHOLDER

John Wainwright

ST. MARTIN'S PRESS
NEW YORK

by the same author

THE HARD HIT
SQUARE DANCE
DEATH OF A BIG MAN
LANDSCAPE WITH VIOLENCE
ACQUITTAL
WHO GOES NEXT?
THE BASTARD
POOL OF TEARS
A NEST OF RATS
DO NOTHIN' TILL YOU HEAR FROM ME
THE JURY PEOPLE
THIEF OF TIME
A RIPPLE OF MURDERS
BRAINWASH
DUTY ELSEWHERE

Copyright © 1980 by John and Avis Wainwright
All rights reserved. For information, write:
St. Martin's Press, Inc. 175 Fifth Ave., New York, N.Y. 10010
Manufactured in the United States of America

Library of Congress Cataloging in Publication Data
Wainwright, John William, 1921-
    The eye of the beholder.

    I. Title.
PZ4.W1418Ey 1980   [PR6073.A354]   823'.914   79-2371
ISBN 0-312-27920-5

Oh! dreadful is the check – intense the agony –
When the ear begins to hear, and the eye begins to see;
When the pulse begins to throb, the brain to think again;
The soul to feel the flesh, and the flesh to feel the chain.

The Prisoner
Emily Brontë

FIRST GLIMPSE

Nor public flame, nor private, dares to shine;
Nor human spark is left, nor glimpse divine!

The Dunciad
Alexander Pope

The Great Gordano made his exit with a flourish, which, fifteen years previously, he would have approved. The 'stage set' of his departure had the subdued luxury which over the years had become his hallmark; elegantly styled drapes, colour without gaudiness, an impression of wealth without brashness. He even had an audience.

He tipped the rum-and-pep down his throat, returned the glass to the side-table by his elbow, seemed about to say something, then flopped forward in his wheelchair and sprawled awkwardly on the thick-piled carpet . . . and the trick was complete.

He was quite dead.

'What so far?'

The detective chief superintendent asked the question, then drew his open hands down the sides of his face, as if to wipe away the last memory of the function from which he'd been called. He was still wearing a dinner jacket, complete with cummerbund and patent leather shoes. He was aware that the growing phalanx of coppers – uniformed and C.I.D. – were viewing his dress with varying degrees of contempt or envy. Screw 'em! When (*if*) any of them reached his own elevated position in the force, they'd know. Dressing up like a monkey's uncle and having to listen through never-ending speeches given by members of The Law Society's local branch was no perk. Forensic jokes – forensic *non*-jokes – gave him a pain. Nor had the dinner been much to write home about and the plonk, which passed as wine, had reminded him of old fashioned red ink.

He said, 'What so far?'

The detective inspector glanced at his open notebook before he spoke.

Then he said, 'George Gordon. Late fifties, early sixties – we haven't established which yet. Potassium cyanide, at a guess. The bitter almonds give-away. The doc agrees.'

'Quick,' observed the detective chief superintendent.

'According to the textbooks almost instantaneous.'

'You think murder?'

The question carried mild surprise.

'Could be suicide.' The detective inspector spoke carefully. 'At the moment, I'd say suspicious circumstances.'

'Why?'

'A bit of a party. Wife, Ruth Gordon. Partner, Neil Baxter. Baxter's wife. John Hector, Frank Dobson, Raymond Dearden – friends. All there when he croaked. All saw it happen. He'd been drinking rum-and-peps most of the evening. His favourite tipple. Not much apparently. Just one too many . . . rum-pep-and-cyanide.'

'No note?'

'Nothing to even suggest suicide.' The detective inspector glanced at the vehicles which filled the U-shaped drive and spilled onto the road. 'That's why the weight. Assuming the worst. Six possible suspects. We have the glass, the rum decanter and bottle, and the bottle of peppermint cordial. Dabs . . . maybe. And six men detailed – four detective constables and a couple of uniformed constables – to look busy, but each keep an eye on one of the "possibles".'

'Why me?' The detective chief superintendent touched his bow-tie self-consciously. 'You seem to have things well under control.'

'Baxter,' murmured the detective inspector.

'What about Baxter?'

10

'He's a friend of the chief.'

'So?'

'I – er – I want a personal search. All six of them. I think it's called for.'

'Neil Baxter,' mused the detective chief superintendent.

'He's an accountant. Partner of the dead man. Lots of things.'

'Including the chief constable's friend?'

'A man of some standing in the local community.' The detective's voice was flat and without emotion. 'If he cuts up rough . . . I'm only an inspector.'

'Whereas *I'm* a chief superintendent.'

'Head of C.I.D.'

'I still take orders from the chief.'

'If he's allowed to *get* to the chief.'

'Mmm.' The detective chief superintendent made the noise as he rubbed his mouth meditatively. He said, 'Suspicious circumstances . . . that's tantamount to sitting on the fence, inspector. Neither murder nor the other thing. A term of art. No . . . not even that. A phrase invented to titillate the press. It means damn-all.'

The detective inspector hesitated, then took a deeper-than-usual breath and said, 'All right. Suspected murder.'

'Good.' The detective chief superintendent smiled. 'That sounds much more positive. We'll go inside and break the news.'

THE DETECTIVE INSPECTOR

His name was Skeel. David Anthony Skeel. Fifteen years, thereabouts, in the Police Service had worked their inverted magic upon his personality; inverted because, as with some men (as with Skeel), the magic had been one of non-transformation. He was the same man and the same sort of man who

11

had been measured for his first uniform. In fifteen years most men change. They become more sure of themselves. They grow more tolerant or more tetchy. Their experience widens and this in turn tends to make them more complete human beings. Thus most men. Indeed thus all men . . . unless they are like Skeel and unless they become policemen.

Skeel had allowed the force to stunt his mental growth. Where other officers – and officers holding lower rank – chanced their arm occasionally, Skeel took no chances. If there was an authorised 'right' way in which to handle any situation, that was the way taken by Skeel. And always had been.

He cut no corners, he did everything 'by the book' and, by so doing, had earned himself the reputation of reliability. The reputation had stood him in good stead; it had ensured progression from beat constable to beat sergeant, from beat sergeant to detective sergeant and, eventually, to his present rank of detective inspector.

The peculiarity was that this reputation for reliability had, at the same time, spawned a counter-reputation for unreliability. His fellow-officers were never at ease when working alongside him. There was no fire in his belly; his own well-being – his own safety – took preference over everything and he refused to close his eyes to even minor irregularities.

He didn't know it (other than in extreme circumstances no officer is allowed to see the contents of his Personal File), but he'd already reached the zenith of his police career. His present companion, the detective chief superintendent, had killed any hope of further promotion via the colloquialism, 'When things get rough this officer can't carry corn'.

It was a succinct summing up of Skeel's shortcomings.

Murder, for example. Skeel had handled other murder enquiries, but in the past they'd been bish-bash-bosh jobs; the blunt instrument, the knife, the firearm. In the main they'd been 'domestic murders'; family squabbles which had ended in a killing.

This however (if indeed it was murder) was a poison caper. Something new. A dimension he'd never touched before. And, more than that, a more-or-less-locked-room set-up. Six suspects. Well seven, if you counted the au pair nurse who at the time of the killing had been upstairs in her own room. A classical 'Agatha Christie' situation. But this time for real.

If, that is, it was murder.

Skeel led the way into the library. A large book-lined room with a refectory table running the centre of its length; with armchairs and sofas and strategically placed stand-lamps; with a high, broad and domed window at one end and with the thick, floor-length curtains pulled back to allow light from the room to filter into part of the garden.

Despite the ten people already present, the room was big enough not to be overcrowded.

'Mrs Gordon?' Skeel asked the question to a uniformed constable standing near the door.

The P.C. said, 'She's with Sergeant Thomas, sir. I think he's taking a statement.'

'Ah.' Skeel nodded his satisfaction, then spoke to the others. 'Ladies. Gentlemen. This is Detective Chief Superintendent Pilter. We've – er – we've decided to treat this incident as murder . . . suspected murder. To be on the safe side.'

Pilter noticed the plural pronoun. 'We' . . . not Skeel. The D.I. was unbolting the exit door, ready for a quick getaway, should that become necessary.

'Murder?'

The question was asked by the tall, hawk-nosed man with becomingly grey side-wings to his immaculately trimmed hair.

'To be on the safe side, sir,' emphasised Skeel.

'And you agree, chief superintendent?'

Pilter drawled, 'I don't disagree. It would seem you *do* disagree.'

'Six of us,' said the tall man.

'So my inspector informs me.'

The tall man's eyes hardened a little and he said, 'My name's Baxter. Neil Baxter.'

Pilter smiled.

'Your chief constable knows me . . . well.'

Pilter murmured, 'I'm sure that must be very pleasant for my chief constable.'

'No.' Baxter frowned. 'What I'm getting at is . . .'

'What *I'm* getting at,' interrupted Pilter, 'is that this case is now one of suspected murder. Suspected poisoning. As you've so rightly pointed out . . . six. Six very obvious suspects. That, I fear, means a search. A personal search. More than that even, a body search.'

'Hey, man, you're not gonna . . .'

'What?'

Pilter turned to face his new protagonist. A young man dressed in expensive jeans and a towelling shirt opened to the waist. He wore the accoutrements of his generation; a thin chain around his neck from which dangled a large medallion; a gold bangle around his left wrist; a single drop earring in the left ear which played peekaboo with the fine blond shoulder-length hair.

He said, 'Nobody's gonna shove his finger up my ass.'

'Nobody,' agreed Pilter. 'But they're going to *look*.'

'The hell they are.'

'Shove it, Slam.'

The third man to speak was perhaps half a decade older than the man he referred to as 'Slam'. He sported a neatly trimmed beard. He too wore an open-necked shirt; this time of nylon and not unbuttoned as low as his companion's. His outstanding feature was the brilliant blueness of his eyes.

He turned to Pilter and said, 'Hector. John Hector.'

Pilter nodded acknowledgement.

Baxter said, 'Chief superintendent, I feel I must object.'

The slim, elegant woman – the woman whose undeniable beauty had (equally undoubtably) been paid for by the square inch – purred, '*You* object! What about me?'

'Darling,' said Baxter, 'you'll no doubt enjoy the experience.'

CELIA BAXTER

The number of times she'd asked herself; the number of times she'd sought an answer to what was essentially a very stupid question. What the hell had she seen in him? What the hell had she ever seen in him?

He was sophisticated and she'd always liked sophisticated men. Okay, he was sophisticated, but it was a very nasty sort of sophistication. It didn't include good manners. It didn't include good behaviour. Dammit, it didn't even include basic decency.

Like now . . .

Out there in the lounge George was still where he'd fallen. Still there. Dead. Surrounded by ham-fisted, big-booted policemen. George . . . the guy he'd so often described as 'the man who made me'. If he'd ever had a friend – assuming the self-opinionated bastard had ever understood the meaning of the word 'friendship' – George had been his friend.

A dead friend. And he didn't give a spit-in-the-wind damn. What the hell had she ever seen in him?

He'd been a womaniser. That was to his credit – the one and only thing he could ever put a tick against – he'd never lied. She'd known. Before their marriage she'd known all about his bed-warming. But like every other dumb dame she'd been sure. So damn sure! She'd change all that; she'd turn him

15

into a home bird; in no time flat she'd make him a pipe-and-slippers man.

Holy mother o' God!

If anything he'd become worse. Nor had he hidden the fact . . . or even tried to hide it.

That face of his. That Roman hooter. That tanned, masculine look. And as age crept up on him, those blasted greying temples. Other men accepted the middle years; lowered the juice a little; worried about their arteries and their ulcers. But not him. All he'd done was change from a young ram into a middle-aged ram, and sometimes with chicks young enough to be his own daughter.

Some clown had once said something about people being able to get used to anything. A male clown, that was for sure. One thing a woman could never 'get used to'. Right? And this hound of a husband of hers knew that score too. He knew how hard it hit her when he slept around. He knew, but he didn't bloody care.

And now, George.

Sweet Jesus . . . poor old George.

From – what was it? – a 'tax consultant'. An accountant – and not even a chartered accountant – a man born with the gift to make figures sit up and beg. From that to The Gordon Agency. From moderate affluence, to big-time spending; from rabbit fur to mink; from a modest semi to a socking great farm, complete with pedigree herd.

And George was stiffening in the next room. And this bastard was still putting on the 'big man' act. And would do. And would continue to do so. Yeah and, despite everything, would continue the rutting session with Ruth. Like knives. Like crazy. Like nothing had ever happened.

And why?

Because he was the biggest louse . . . ever.

She said, 'My husband is very proficient at making foul remarks. It comes with years of practice.'

Skeel began, 'It's quite all right, Mrs Baxter. In the . . .'

'You'll be searched, madam.' Pilter interrupted Skeel. 'We have policewomen. You may, if you wish, have a nurse present.'

'There's the *au pair* nurse,' murmured Skeel.

'Her,' agreed Pilter. 'Or any other nurse you care to call. The men may have their own doctor present. We'll make it as – er – painless as possible. But it's necessary.'

'Search warrants, are *they* necessary?'

The man wearing the cravat asked the question. He was slim to the point of gauntness. Pale, almost unhealthy-looking. Relaxed enough to give the impression of a deliberate pose. He wore a wine-coloured jacket, a navy-blue shirt and flared, army-twill trousers.

'Cool it, Ray.' Hector's startlingly blue eyes glinted a warning.

'A reasonable question.' Pilter smiled at the pale man. 'The answer is no, we don't need a warrant. For anything. Murder's been committed. We start from that assumption. From that reasonable suspicion. Short of physical violence to the obviously innocent anything goes. And none of you people are yet *obviously* innocent.'

The pale man said, 'I always thought innocent until proved guilty.'

'In court,' said Pilter. 'Before the hearing – suspected until proved innocent. There's quite a difference.'

'Five of us,' mused Baxter.

'Six.' His wife corrected him.

'Ruth's hardly likely to . . .'

'Women *have* been known to kill their husbands.' She flashed a hard, tight smile. 'Some have one hell of a motive . . . sweetheart.'

17

THE DETECTIVE CHIEF SUPERINTENDENT

Thomas Pilter . . . Head of C.I.D.

Which meant can-carrier-in-chief. Which meant he'd better keep a tight rein on this quintet of weirdos. They were too flash by half. All of them. Poisoning. Murder – at the very least suspected murder – and nobody was over-excited. Nobody was over-concerned. Nobody was over-anything.

The pompous prat. The I-know-people-in-high-places nut. Well . . . could be. Could be he was a drinking buddy of the chief's. On the other hand could be he'd once said 'Excuse me' to the chief when passing him on the way to the slash-house. Technically it made no difference. Theoretically it didn't mean a damn thing. But in practice!

The Old Pals Act had not yet been rescinded. Nor ever would be.

And his missus. The slinky, brittle bint. That one had 'Trouble' spelled out in neon lighting all over her hot little carcass. She could return hatred with all the ease of a brick wall bouncing back a tennis ball. She had claws, and she could use them.

The bearded boy. The blue-eyed beauty. Very cool. Very sure of himself. A subtle, not-too-obvious arrogance. Something which just might up and smack somebody not waiting for it in the teeth. At a guess a lad used to having his own way.

And the pale-faced creep. A nancy-boy . . . what else? A homo. A one-in-every-twenty screwball. Ah well, this was a very modern and permissive society. So that couldn't be held against him.

But . . .

Poofters could turn very nasty sometimes. They were incomplete men; men who occasionally had all the worst traits of women in their make-up. The gay crowd knew how to

18

create aggro . . . so watch your step with that one, Pilter, old son.

And the other one? The 'with it' chump they called 'Slam'?

Just that . . . a chump. Medallions, earrings and hairy chests usually meant damn-all inside. A nothing. One to make the number up. Maybe the odd man out, and if so why so?

As sweet a bunch of flowers as any copper could wish for. Take your pick, Pilter. If it is murder take your pick . . . any one of 'em.

When she entered the room Pilter thought he recognised her; thought he'd seen her before. Just for a moment he thought he knew her, or should have known her. Then the penny dropped.

She was a softer, less quartz-like edition of Baxter's wife. A few years older, perhaps. Or if not older, if not *much* older, less anxious to hide her true age. The hair was liberally speckled with grey. The cosmetics were not as skilfully applied. The foundation garments were less constricting.

A detective constable followed her into the library and closed the door against the sound of official movement beyond.

Skeel stepped towards her and said, 'Mrs Gordon. This is Detective Chief Superintendent Pilter.'

Pilter moved his head in acknowledgement of the introduction.

Baxter's wife placed her arm across the woman's shoulders and, as she led her to a chair, said, 'It's being treated as murder, Ruth. They're mad . . . of course they're mad. But that's how the official mind works.'

The woman was quite composed. She lowered herself into the chair and if she didn't quite relax there was, at least, no visual sign of numbing grief.

Pilter said, 'Suspected murder, Mrs Gordon. Subject to final verification by the pathologist and the toxicologist –

your husband was poisoned. We think – again subject to verification – potassium cyanide.'

She said, 'Please feel free, superintendent. You have a duty. It won't be obstructed in this house. Ask your questions. Do all the searching you think necessary.'

'You're distraught, my poor darling.' Baxter crossed the room to join his wife and Ruth Gordon. 'You don't know what you're saying.'

'If they wish to search. If they think . . .'

'A personal search. A *body* search.' Celia Baxter's painted mouth moved into a scarlet sneer. 'Lover-man doesn't like the idea. He probably forgot to change his underpants before he came.'

'Celia . . . please!'

For the first time emotion showed on the face of the recently created widow. Not sadness. Not shock. Nothing which might have sprung from the fact of her husband's death. But a frown of mild disgust; a look of censure at the other woman's inability to hide, or even try to hide, the contempt she had for her husband.

NEIL BAXTER

The wrong woman, that was the trouble. He'd married the wrong woman. The wrong sister. This expensive tart he had as a wife lacked even basic good manners.

She was also dumb. Unbelievably dumb.

'Love'. Jesus, she still believed in the stupid lyrics spewed out by the writers of pop songs. Moon-and-June crap. Happy-ever-after garbage. At her age for Christ's sake!

He knew women. Women were his speciality. His hobby. One might almost describe it as his art.

And if it was his art – if he'd elevated the act of copulation into an art form – damnation, no artist paints the same scene

20

over and over again. So simple. So obvious. He needed a continual supply of new canvasses. He needed them, otherwise he'd become old and stale and, in time, as useless as a castrated tom.

Figure it out.

The great lovers of history. Forget Casanova, assuming he was ever more than a myth, he was just a shagging machine. No. Think of the greats. Napoleon. The magnificent monarchs of the past. The original Prince Regent. Some of the late – and not so late – presidents of America. Yeah, religious leaders, too. Think of them. And remember most of them were married.

So what? They were married.

But to good women. To wise and understanding women. To women who knew that with a man – with a complete man – masculinity was what made him great. To women who had the sense to realise that such a man had more animal virility than any one woman could satisfy; that to reach his potential in other fields he had also to satisfy a basic requirement.

Odd. He'd thought Celia – Celia of all the women he'd ever slept with – would understand these things. That was the impression she'd given. That was the impression she'd meant to give.

The impression . . . until the ring was on her finger.

After that she'd become possessive. Fast! As if she'd bought him. As if she could satisfy him forever. The same bloody canvas. The same bloody scene. God Almighty . . . she'd believed that.

Pop-song lyrics. Moon-and-June crap.

No way, friend, no bloody way.

Skeel murmured, 'There's a policewoman sergeant standing by, sir.'

'Good.' Pilter nodded his satisfaction. He turned to the

half a dozen 'suspects' and said, 'That's it then, ladies and gentlemen. One at a time. We'll use a bedroom.'

'The main bedroom,' suggested Ruth Gordon. 'There's an en suite bathroom, toilet and shower . . . if needed.'

'Thank you, ma'am.' Pilter favoured her with a quick smile of appreciation. He continued, 'Inspector Skeel will accompany the gentlemen, one at a time. There'll also be a detective sergeant. If anybody wants one of his friends to be present – or as I've said a doctor – there are no objections.' He paused and watched their faces. The man 'Slam' scowled his displeasure; gentle amusement danced in the blue brilliance of Hector's eyes; the others remained stonefaced and silent. Pilter continued, 'The two ladies. They can go together if they wish. That's their choice.'

'Singly.' Celia Baxter spoke the word with a finality which dismissed all argument.

'One at a time, then,' agreed Pilter. 'There's a policewoman sergeant who'll replace Inspector Skeel. There's also, I understand, an *au pair* nurse somewhere in the house.'

'Hulda,' murmured Ruth Gordon.

'She can be present. Or a nurse – or doctor – of your own choice. And there'll be a policewoman constable present.' Pilter paused for reaction or complaint. None came and he continued, 'Ladies, I would like you to take your handbags with you. Everybody to take their outer clothes with them. please, collect them on the way. Then I'm sorry, but you must strip to the skin. Every pocket – every handbag – emptied. Keys, cash, personal papers – letters and so forth – will be returned. Everything else will be taken into police possession against receipt. Your clothes, of course, will be returned to you after the body search.' Once more he paused, then in a quieter tone added, 'There'll be as little inconvenience as possible. You have my assurance. We *should* take possession of the clothes. We won't. Instead, we'll take a sample of whatever dust happens to be in the bottom of the pockets –

the handbags – wherever dust accumulates, including the inside and soles of the shoes.' He looked directly at Baxter as he ended, 'Any cause for complaint – anything which embarrasses or upsets you – let me know. Or, failing that, let my chief constable know.'

Celia Baxter's voice was low and contemptuous as she said, 'And don't think the idiot won't.'

There was a silence. One of those awkward waiting silences in which each glanced self-consciously at the others and waited for the first volunteer.

The man called 'Slam' put a hand inside the wide open towelling of his shirt and rubbed his ribs. Slowly. As if wishing to make some sort of movement and only being able to think of this one rather stupid gesture of puny non-defiance.

Beneath the beard Hector's mouth bent into a twisted smile.

As he unfolded himself from the chair he said, 'Okay. I'll be first.'

'Thank you.'

Pilter stood aside to allow Hector to pass. A detective constable followed Hector then after the D.C. Skeel, who closed the library door as they left.

JOHN HECTOR

One way out of the meat-grinder . . . wouldn't you say? Grandpa with the scythe cancelled all contracts. Even Gordon Agency contracts.

Maybe. Maybe not. But sure as hell it was worth a try. With George reduced to haunting old houses the agency folded, or should fold. Baxter had only been there as moving furniture; a yum-yum to make the office look lived-in. With George gone . . . no way.

So? Okay, George had been that first fuse necessary to

23

*send The Ectoplasm into orbit. He'd organised the first dates.
The first big dates. But what hadn't been there George
couldn't have put there. All he'd done was recognise it. All
he'd done was shove it in the right shop-window. After that
people had bought. People had paid – paid good – but always
through George.*

And (if the contract held water) for ever and ever amen.

Well, screw that for a bowl of cherries.

*The Ectoplasm had it. That extra something. That golden
thread between 'good' and 'great'. Like The Beatles. Like
The Stones. Like every other group capable of playing everlasting yo-yo in the Top Ten. And The Ectoplasm had that
extra something.*

*But George had wanted to – what was his goofy phrase? –
'Keep it clean. Lose the dope label'.*

*Mac, these days 'clean' numbers weren't even square. They
were cubic. The words of every good number carried a message. The same message. The today song-smiths didn't write
boy-and-girl things. They wrote boy-girl-and-bed words. Bang
numbers. That or Jesus Christ numbers. What the kids
wanted the kids had to have, and that was what the kids
wanted. Kinky? Okay, kinky. But only a nut criticised the
coin-making combination.*

Which made George a nut.

*And what was weed, anyway? What was a little grass?
Nobody was onto the heavy stuff. Nobody was main-lining.
A stick here, a stick there – a little like lighting up a cancer-
tube, a damn sight safer that lighting up a cancer-tube. Come
soon it had to be made legal. Nothing surer. The soft stuff.
Too many kids puffed it . . . it had to be made legal.*

*So George was a nut – had been a nut – but George carried
a very heavy contract, had carried a very heavy contract.
But no more, mac. When he'd tipped out of that wheelchair
of his all contracts had been cancelled.*

And boy, this was real freedom.

24

This was where The Ectoplasm started riding the real wave. When all the other groups fought for second spot.

Skeel dropped the receiver onto its rest and in a voice low enough not to reach the other occupants of the library said, 'The lab liaison officer. It *was* potassium cyanide. Traces still in the glass.'

'Quick,' murmured Pilter.

'It's a very simple chemical test. They knew what they were looking for.'

'Fine.' Pilter jerked the bow-tie loose, then he moved his hands to the back of his waist in order to unbuckle the cummerbund as he watched the policewoman sergeant guide Celia Baxter from the library. He said, 'Somewhere private. It's time we asked some questions.'

'There's an office . . . of a sort. Gordon's office. Poky.'

'Good. That makes for confidentiality. Where is it?'

'Next door.' Skeel moved his head. 'Next to this place.'

'Keep the others occupied. I'll take the lists with me.' Pilter held out a hand and Skeel passed the tabulated details of what the search had found in each man's pockets. Pilter said, 'We'll start with Dopey . . . the one they call "Slam".'

'Dobson,' said Skeel.

'That his name?'

'Do you want me to come . . .'

'No. Nobody. Some personal feeling-out. That for starters.' Pilter glanced down at his hands. One held the papers. The other held the cummerbund. He draped the cummerbund over Skeel's arm and said, 'Hang on to this infernal thing. And don't let 'em play footsie with each other.' He walked towards the body of the library – towards the youngest man in the room – and said, 'Dobson.'

'Eh!' The single pendant from his left ear swung as he jerked his head.

'A few words,' said Pilter.

25

'What about?'

'This and that.'

'Hey, man . . .'

'Not here,' interrupted Pilter.

'Hey . . . what is this?' Dobson's voice was harsh. It held fear. Perhaps panic. He flicked his eyes at the others, then looked directly at the bearded man.

Hector murmured, 'Cool it, kid.'

'It ain't you they're gonna . . .'

'Eventually,' soothed Pilter.

'What?'

'Everybody eventually. But you first.'

'Why me?'

'Why not?'

'For Christ's sake! I didn't . . .'

'In that case,' said Pilter, 'why all the sweat?'

'I ain't sweating.'

'Good.' Pilter moved his head. 'There's an office next door. On your feet, sonny. Let's have a chat.'

FRANK 'SLAM' DOBSON

When a man's life starts being unstitched. When a man's whole future depends upon some old coot being stiffened. Man, that was not too easy to live with. That was definitely not a very nice ball game.

So who wanted to go back to square one? Who wanted the back streets of Huddersfield again? Who wanted a lush for a father and a whore for a mother? Who wanted to have to lift things from the supermarket shelves in order to eat?

Who?

Don't hatch eggs pondering the question, man. One answer, that's all. One simple answer. Not 'Slam' Dobson.

He could hit the skins. Okay he was no Buddy Rich, but

26

who the hell was? Nevertheless he could use the sticks well enough to drive the group on a straight rail. The Ectoplasm. A kinky name if ever there was one, but Hector had to have his handle attached and Hector was the man with the ideas. Hector also hankered after bread. Lots and lots of bread. Maybe too much bread. Maybe that was the one thing wrong with the guy.

Nevertheless ...

Old man Gordon had been hinting at another drummer for too long. And what the hell did he know about drumming, anyway? Groups needed drummers. Not fancy drummers like once-upon-a-time. Loud drummers. Drummers who could slam the skins loud enough to bounce the beat higher than amplified guitar strings. That's all – that and a little flash, that's all.

And now everything was okay. The Ectoplasm still had a drummer and the name of that drummer was 'Slam' Dobson. The Hector boy would be out front, mauling the mike and giving with the vocals. The rest of the gang would be shoving fancy chords and tricky rip-offs through the speakers. The coloured lights would be flashing and spinning, and the chicks would be drooling at the edges. But – man – right there in the basement, holding the whole fantastic zing-zang in one piece, would be old 'Slam' Dobson ... beating those skins like crazy and making the whole joint ride high and handsome.

'Correct me if I'm wrong,' smiled Pilter. 'These days they call them "joints".'

'Eh?' Dobson stared. For the moment he seriously thought Pilter was capable of mind-reading.

'In the old days they were called "vipers".'

'I dunno what the hell . . .'

'Before your time, of course. Same stuff, though. Resin of hemp.' He smiled. 'Odd. It doesn't sound too heroic when it's given its real name, does it? Sounds like smoking rope-ends.'

Dobson looked hurt.

It was, as Skeel had warned, a particularly small room. A real one-man office. A table-desk fixed to one wall. One modern armchair, presumably for visitors. An oak-veneered filing cabinet. A corner cupboard containing drinks. Very compact; very intimate; very . . . claustrophobic perhaps. Warm enough – close enough – to bring the sheen of sweat to Dobson's face.

Pilter had hoisted one buttock onto the desk and from there he gazed down at the younger man as he sprawled in the armchair.

'You had . . .' Pilter checked the list in his hand. 'You had five – er – "joints" in your possession. Right?'

'I thought,' snarled Dobson, 'this was a murder enquiry.'

'Broadly speaking,' agreed Pilter.

'So? I'm gonna be dropped for holding some soft stuff?'

'More than likely. We're always grateful for small mercies.'

'Jeeze!' Dobson almost spat. 'You creeps know how to . . .'

'But not necessarily,' said Pilter very slowly. Very deliberately.

'Uh?' Dobson stared.

'Did *you* kill him?' asked Pilter in a quiet, conversational tone.

'Hey . . . what the hell?'

'Did you?'

'I ain't gonna sit here and be made the fall . . .'

'Answer the damn question.' The switch in tone caught Dobson flat-footed. 'Did *you* kill Gordon?'

'No . . . I did not. Any creep says I did is a . . .'

'I know. A liar.'

'Yeah. One hell of a liar. Why should I kill the old guy?'

28

'Why should anybody?' Pilter's tone had reverted back to one of near-boredom.

'Ask *me*.' Dobson spread his palms.

'Thanks . . . I will.'

'Eh?'

'Why should anybody kill Gordon?'

'I dunno. How would I know?'

'You think he died a natural death?' suggested Pilter innocently.

'The hell he died a natural death.'

'I wasn't there. You were. What happened?'

'Somebody poisoned the old gink.'

'Just like that?'

'Yeah, I guess.'

Pilter smiled and said, 'I'm not prepared to believe you're such a brainless mug, Dobson.'

'Eh?'

'Y'know . . . "just like that".'

'I – er – I guess they had a reason,' muttered Dobson.

' "They"?'

'Whoever shoved poison into him.'

'Who?'

'How the hell do I . . .'

'These things.' Pilter tapped the list gently with the nail of a forefinger.

'Eh?'

'Five – er – "sticks".'

'For Chrissake!'

'Nothing for nothing, old son.' Pilter paused, then added, 'The world isn't built that way.'

'What do I know?' pleaded Dobson. 'What the hell am I *supposed* to know?'

'Who didn't like him?' asked Pilter gently.

'Gordon?'

'Who didn't like him?' repeated Pilter.

29

Dobson hesitated. Pilter allowed him ample time to think; to weigh the odds; to appreciate his own position; to remember the minor illegality he had been caught out on.

Pilter lighted a cigarette and smoked it patiently as he waited.

'Okay.' Dobson moved his shoulders resignedly. 'The old creep wasn't too popular.'

'Specifically?' encouraged Pilter.

Dobson said, 'He ran this agency . . . see? The Gordon Agency. Baxter was his side-kick. His buddy, but that didn't mean much. Gordon was ace man. And he tied people up. Tight.'

'Tell me about the agency,' said Pilter.

'Y'know . . . performers. Groups. Stand-up comics. Anything the northern circuit could use. He had the in with the club crowd. The big clubs. He gave them acts . . . see? Strippers. Drags. Groups. Anything. They buzzed him, he gave 'em the acts.'

'And the contracts were tight?'

'Tight as a nun's ass,' said Dobson with feeling.

'Go on.'

'Well, Johnny – Johnny Hector. He had some great ideas about The Ectoplasm. He . . .'

'The Ectoplasm?'

'The group. I drum the group.'

'I see. Go on.'

'We could make the goldies, see? We could climb. But Gordon wouldn't hear. He wanted the same old crap. He wanted safe. No chances. And Hector leaned the other way and wanted out.'

'And?'

'No way.' Dobson shook his head. 'The old man's mind was in concrete. Even his old lady couldn't move him.'

'His wife?'

'She ain't bad.' Dobson made the observation as if it was

30

a considered opinion, arrived at after much thought. 'She ain't young, but she ain't bad.'

'She was on your side? On Hector's side?'

'Well now,' Dobson moved his hands. 'She ain't really on key. At that age, what else? But – y'know – open to persuasion.'

'Against her husband's better judgement?'

'It ain't his better judgement . . . *wasn't*. He knew all from hell, see? He was back in the hurdy-gurdy days. These clubs. They ain't *clubs* any more. Y'know, what used to be clubs. They come lush and expensive these days. They pay good, they want the best. Man. you get top names billing there. All we made was second-spot . . . top-spot, maybe, on the second string circuit. We wanted best. That's what the aggro was about. And Gordon wouldn't listen. His old lady, though. Y'know . . .

RUTH GORDON

She felt guilty. She felt guilty, because she felt nothing. No real sorrow. No real loss. No real shock. Therefore she felt guilty.

He'd been a good man. Not an easy man to live with; not a passive, uncomplaining man. But despite that, a good man.

Nor did the thought of the Neil Baxter thing ease her feeling of guilt.

Those first years of their marriage. They'd been good years. Complete years. They'd loved each other . . . physically, too. But not just that. That had been only a part of it. The bedroom part; an important part, but not the most important part.

Then after the accident. The wheelchair. And the love had still been there. They'd both known that . . . that the love was still there as strong as ever. And for a while . . .

Dear God, within the privacy of their bedroom, they'd tried. How they'd tried. How he'd tried. For nothing. For efforts and experiments which had left them both with a feeling of shame.

And he'd said, 'You need a man, Ruth. A complete man.'

'For God's sake!' The voicing of what she'd known to be the truth had shocked her.

'I need you.' The gentle solemnity of his words had brought the prickle of tears behind her eyes. 'For companionship. For somebody to hang onto. But you're still young. Healthy. Normal. Stay with me, Ruth. That's all I ask. For the other thing . . . find another man. Just don't love him. That's all I ask.'

He'd been right, of course. The urges – the natural functionings – had been there. And (of course) Celia's husband had been there. There and anxious.

Neil. The perfect copulating machine. The immaculate answer to their problem. Nobody could love Neil. Even Celia didn't love Neil . . . she merely tolerated him.

A crazy set-up. Something the scandal-rags could have made into a centre-page spread. And yet . . .

George knew; knew and approved. Celia knew; knew and accepted; accepted because Neil was a ram and always would be a ram, and it was perhaps a little less humiliating when the 'other woman' wasn't really important – wasn't out for a catch – and, furthermore, was her own sister.

Celia had even said, 'We don't get bitchy with each other about men, darling. Especially about men like Neil. Go ahead . . . keep it in the family. George might not mind as much.'

Neil?

Neil, she supposed, had never even guessed at the truth. He was far too self-centred to think it as other than a conquest. He was a great one at self-delusion. He thought they were 'lovers'. They weren't. They were 'lusters' . . . assuming

32

such a word existed. Whether or not it did, it described their relationship to perfection.

And George?

George never broke a promise. All his life he'd never broken a promise. Therefore he'd accepted. He'd suggested . . . therefore he'd accepted. But as time had passed he'd had regrets. Inside he'd hurt. Inside he'd wept. And in spite of all things she'd always been close enough to know . . . everything.

And yet she felt guilty. Guilty . . . because she felt nothing.

Pilter swung his free leg, inhaled cigarette smoke, and said, 'Not a party, then?'

'Party?' Dobson looked puzzled.

'This get-together. Seven of you. Not, strictly speaking, a party?'

'Sort of,' muttered Dobson.

'Meaning?'

'Well . . . y'know.'

'No. Tell me.'

'Every night. Most nights. Old man Gordon liked company, I guess. People gathered. Were asked. People from his stable. Food. A few drinks. A rabbit about how things were going. What was gonna happen next. His way of keeping checks, I guess.'

'A sort of social-cum-business affair.'

'Yeah.' Dobson nodded.

'What about . . . what's his name?' Pilter consulted his lists. 'Dearden. What about him?'

'The poofter?' Dobson smirked.

'It's pretty obvious,' said Pilter. 'It takes more than that to shock me. I'm asking. Where does he fit in?'

'Official snapshot man.'

'Photographer?'

'Yeah.' Almost reluctantly Dobson added, 'He makes good pictures.'

'Of the people under contract to Gordon?'

'Yeah . . . I guess.'

'Just the odd man out?' suggested Pilter.

'Eh?'

'Tonight. Hector and yourself, part of this Ectoplasm group. Gordon and Baxter. The two wives. Dearden . . . the odd man out.'

'He's a queer. I told you.'

'I'm sorry.' Pilter frowned. 'Let's assume I'm dumb.'

'Dearden. Hector. They share the same pad.'

'Aah!'

'Except when we're on the road. One-night gigs, that sorta thing. Except that, they're – y'know – "married".'

'Quite a collection,' observed Pilter quietly.

'Eh?'

'The six of you. We can forget Gordon. He's no longer with us. But the rest of you. Tell me, what did Gordon think of the Hector–Dearden relationship?'

'He just guessed. He wasn't dumb.'

'And?'

'What d'you think?'

Pilter squashed what was left of the cigarette into an ash-tray by his right hip.

He murmured, 'To be honest I'm almost past thinking anything.'

'He blew his gasket every few days,' said Dobson.

'Not broad-minded in other words?'

'Hey, man, that old boy was hard. You hear me? He had us all scared sometimes. Yeah, even Baxter. And Baxter was his partner. No way, though. When Gordon blew steam everybody ducked. That wheelchair and all. He hated the damn thing. That made him hot stuff, whenever he lifted his lid.

34

Okay – the wheelchair, he couldn't kick hell outa *that* so he kicked hell outa anybody else around.'

'Okay.' Pilter pulled the loosened bow-tie from around his neck. As he wound it, bandage-like around one hand, he said, 'Let's move to the mechanics of this thing. The actual he-did-she-did routine.'

'Sorry.' Dobson scowled. 'I don't get . . .'

'He was in his wheelchair?'

'Gordon? Sure. As always.'

Pilter slipped the folded tie into a side pocket of his dinner jacket, and said, 'Rum-and-pep? That right?'

'Yeah. His poison.'

'His favourite drink?'

'His *only* drink. I never knew him drink anything else.'

'His first of the night?'

'Hell, no. His fourth. Maybe his fifth.'

'Who mixed them?'

'He did. I tell you, he was a crazy old coot, nobody else mixed the damn things right.'

'From the wheelchair?'

'Sure. He had this table. Alongside the chair. The rum . . . in a decanter thing. And the pep. A bottle of the stuff. When he wanted one, he mixed one.'

'And the rest of you?'

'His old lady fixed us. Scotch, mostly. The Dearden fink stayed on coke . . . the rest Scotch. Some water, some soda.'

'Mixed by Mrs Gordon?'

'Yeah.'

'Every time?'

'Yeah.' Dobson snapped his fingers, then said, 'Nope. Baxter. He fixed his own drink a coupla times. And maybe once for his woman.'

'I get the sense of movement,' mused Pilter.

'Some,' agreed Dobson.

'You mentioned aggro.'

'Not heavy stuff. Nobody was . . .'

'At least arguments?'

'Yeah, hard talk. This contract thing.'

'Between Hector and Gordon?'

'Everybody was taking sides, man.'

'Sitting down? Walking around?'

'Both . . . I guess.' Dobson held his head to one side as a sign of concentration. The blond hair hung loose and covered the single-drop earring. He said, 'Y'know, sometimes up, sometimes down. Walking around. Waving arms. The way it is.'

'Passing Gordon's wheelchair?'

'Oh, sure. Sure.'

'Passing the side-table?'

'Yeah . . . sure.'

'How bad was this argument?'

'Pretty loud at times, I guess.' Dobson grinned. 'Man, that guy Gordon knew how to needle.'

'The – er – picture.' Pilter seemed to be talking to himself. 'An argument. Seven people. Five men, two women. One of the men in a wheelchair. Movement . . . probably a lot of movement. Except, of course, for the man in the wheelchair. The side-table. The rum. The peppermint cordial. The wine-glass. People passing the table. Then the man in the wheel-chair tipping the rum-and-pep down his throat . . . and that's it.'

'Just about,' agreed Dobson, 'except he sipped the drink a coupla times before he finished it.'

'Sipped it?' Pilter raised an eyebrow.

'Yeah . . . maybe a coupla times. Y'know. The way they do.'

'No ill effects?'

'It didn't make him come off the boil, if that's what you mean.'

'What about the time-lag?'

'Eh?'

'How long? Between him pouring the drink and finishing it?'

'Man . . . how do *I* know? I don't keep no stop-watch . . .'

'Approximately?'

'Maybe half an hour . . . maybe. Okay . . . say half an hour.'

'And all that time people passing his wheelchair? Passing the table with the drink on it?'

'Yeah. I guess. Except the queer.'

'Dearden?'

'He didn't move much. Dearden ain't no ball of fire. He just sits and sulks.'

RAYMOND DEARDEN

So he was 'different'? Effeminate? A 'creature' as opposed to a 'man'?

Great God . . . men!

Gordon had, no doubt, considered himself to be a man. A man for God's sake! Despite being dead from the waist down he'd still thought of himself as a man. Such rubbish. Such pathetic arrogance. Just because he could shout and hurt and humiliate and force his silly opinions upon anybody less noisy than himself.

Manhood . . . for what it was worth.

Well he wasn't a man now, was he? Not even half a man.

Whereas he, Raymond Dearden, was still complete, as he'd always been complete. Himself and, when occasion demanded it, no small force to be reckoned with.

But above all else unique, in that he was an artist; an artist who used cameras and lighting techniques – filters and dark room magic – where other artists used brushes and a canvas.

He was more than a 'photographer'. Much more than that.

37

He created pictures with light and shade. The tonings. The surrounding scenics. The reversals. The solarisations. The themes. His artistry included a complete knowledge – an absolute mastery – of graduations and lens apertures; of emulsions and high spots; of burnings and dodgings.

The result was beauty. Genuine beauty, but lost on men like Gordon.

What was it Gordon had once said?

'Not something to study. Not something to drool over. Something to hit 'em. Something as brash and as eye-searing as headlines. That's what I pay for and that's what I want.'

The words of a moronic fool. The words of a lout who couldn't understand – who would never understand – that the love of a man for another man extended well beyond the back-slapping, mock punch-throwing of adult adolescence.

Love was love . . . period. And the respective sex of the two beings who loved each other was unimportant. Nor could 'dirt' live where love was alive and all-consuming; nor could love – any form of genuine love – be misnamed and called 'perversion'.

Something else Gordon had never understood, and would now never understand.

Gordon was dead.

Who, then, would miss him?

Only the worms must now endure his silent presence.

'A real bumper bundle,' observed Pilter sourly.

'Eh?' The detective chief superintendent was well ahead of the thought-process of Dobson.

'Six of you,' grumbled Pilter. 'And I doubt if there'll be six wreaths.'

'That for sure.' Dobson grinned as he moved into step.

Pilter eased himself from the desk. He shoved his hands into the pockets of his trousers and, as much as the cramped space of the tiny office would allow, walked backwards and forwards as he voiced his thoughts.

He said. 'What the hell was he like, this man Gordon? What was he *really* like? Chair-bound, okay that could have made a difference to his temper. A perfectionist, I get the feeling he was some sort of perfectionist. He liked his own way. He was perhaps a little selfish, but at the same time he boosted the pulling-power of performers listed in his agency. He was no fly-by-night. That's obvious. This place – this life-style – isn't top-dressing. If he could afford this on a percentage . . . that means the people he represented were making money. Good money.' He turned and looked at Dobson. 'That right, so far?'

'Yeah.' There was some reluctance in the agreement. Reluctance, but acceptance. Dobson added, 'He fixed things. He just wanted his own way too much.'

'So far.' Pilter spoke slowly. He moved to the desk, rested the backs of his thighs against the desk top, then continued, 'That's about all, Dobson, for now. Like the rest of 'em, you'll be asked to make a full statement. Tomorrow if possible. At the local nick. I might want to see you again.'

'The – er – the sticks?' muttered Dobson.

'We'll see,' promised Pilter. 'When it's all come out, we'll see. Just don't gamble on it. I want to know a lot more about Gordon before I make any deals.'

FLASHBACK

Magic fascinated him. The conjurer; the illusionist; the professional trickster who in those days could command the full second half of a variety bill – sometimes the complete evening – and with props large enough and numerous enough to need a furniture-van-sized vehicle to transport them from theatre to theatre, worked miracle after miracle, each more breath-taking than the one before. They were his gods. They were his idols. He yearned for far more than the knowledge of 'how it was done' . . . he yearned – almost *ached* – to do it himself.

Obviously, he couldn't remember the great Houdini; that mock-Merlin had killed himself, performing his fabulous Water Torture Cell routine, when George Gordon was only two years old. But in later years, when the magic bug had bitten and when he was consciously directing his own life towards a similar make-believe world, he talked to men and women who had known Harry Houdini. Men and women to whom the greatest escapologist of them all was still a recent memory. He talked and he listened. He learned that the strait-jackets from which Houdini wriggled were no 'trick' affairs; that any man who, like Houdini, could control his muscles and deliberately dislocate his own shoulders, then jerk them back into their sockets, could also disengage himself from this 'impossible' bondage. He learned that, in effect, Houdini had two pairs of hands; that he could manipulate keys and

40

pick locks with his toes as easily – more easily – than most men could with their fingers; that this ability, combined with the practised knack of regurgitation, allowed him to shrug off personal searches, however intimate and thorough, and still leave him with the means and the movement to escape from just about anything.

Houdini. Perhaps the greatest of them all. The man who had turned his own body into a box of tricks. The men and women he talked to and questioned knew how it was done, but only Houdini could ever *do* it.

The trick body had, at last, let him down. He'd thumbed a nose at nature once too often. The strain had been too much and in October 1926 peritonitis had been one straitjacket from which he couldn't escape.

And yet . . . not Houdini. Escapology was after all merely one trick; it could be permutated, it could be guyed up in a hundred different gewgaws, but it remained escapology. And Houdini himself had taken from escapology everything escapology could ever give.

No. He wanted to be a magician; a magician on a grand scale. An illusionist. A man with his own company; with his own tricks which he, personally, had invented and perfected.

By the age of fourteen (1938) Gordon was earning a local reputation at church halls and minor functions around his home as 'The Schoolboy Magician'. He wore a pseudo-Etonian dress, complete with topper and silver-headed cane. His trousers and the 'bum starver' jacket were honeycombed with hidden pockets and already his act had polish and flair. Small magic-box tricks were his forte, but running a close second were card tricks, in which the nimbleness of his fingers was of paramount importance, which brought genuine applause from an audience unused to such 'professionalism' at these functions.

Despite the threat of war, the great names of stage magic

41

still toured the halls. Jasper Maskelyne – son of the great John Nevil Maskelyne – topped the bill at Leeds Empire and via a mutual acquaintance Gordon was introduced to the slim, suave magician in the star's dressing room.

Despite the difference in years their mutual enthusiasm for stage magic sparked an immediate friendship.

'The secret,' smiled Maskelyne, 'is to catch the audience unawares. The perfect trick is the one which every wiseacre watching "knows how it's done". Then when he's puffed himself out with false pride prove that that is *not* the way the trick was done.'

'That's not easy, sir,' said Gordon.

'Oh, yes.' Maskelyne nodded. 'Each trick – almost every trick – can be performed in more than one way. Sawing The Lady In Half. At least half a dozen ways of performing that seemingly impossible feat. They know – the audience – that it can't *be* done. Two ladies . . . one in each half of the cabinet. Very well. Find some way of convincing them that only *one* lady is in the cabinet. A trick saw. One with a false blade. Again, dumbfound them by proving, conclusively, that the blade of the saw is made of fine steel, newly sharpened. The trick – the hardest trick facing any illusionist – is to remain one step ahead of the audience . . . to know what *they're* thinking, then prove them wrong.'

They talked for more than an hour and before he left Maskelyne wrote Gordon a letter of introduction to his father's friend, David Devant, doyen of all British magicians and at that time retired after a nervous breakdown.

The meeting with Maskelyne was a crossroads in Gordon's life. He had now no doubts. He changed his billing and became 'The Young Gordano'. In the summer of that year he pestered his way into one of the lesser seaside touring shows, threw up his job as a clerk in a wine importing firm, withdrew all his meagre savings and turned pro.

There was, of course, the inevitable argument with his

42

parents, but it was not of the usual heroic proportions. They warned him. They advised him against. But when they realised that warnings and advice meant nothing, they resigned themselves, wished him well and assured him of a home to return to should his dreams turn sour.

'The Young Gordano' achieved stature as a minor illusionist; his cabinets became larger and more complex; the mechanics of his various trickeries increased in their intricacy and he was, perhaps, the first stage magician to perfect the double- then triple-tier routine. To make the lady appear out of thin air; to levitate the lady, without visible means of support; to make the lady vanish into thin air from whence she had come. Three tricks in one. Each an applause-puller, but each a distinct part of the same, overall routine.

But if he was a fine and forever improving magician, he was a poor member of a touring company. He refused to 'mix'. He insisted that the wings and the flies be cleared of fellow-performers and back-stage workers once his act was under way; the secrets of his tricks were *his* and he trusted nobody.

The manager of the company tried to make him relax this rule a little.

'Gordon, you can't expect the others to hide behind corners whilever you're on stage.'

'I don't expect it. I demand it.'

'For God's sake, why? You're only a kid conjurer. Some of these people . . .'

'Some of these people,' snapped Gordon, 'have been on the stage all their lives. They're old enough to be my parents. Yet they're second billing to me. And why? Because over the years they've let other people filch their material and build on it. I'll not take that chance. The secrets of my tricks are mine. Some I've bought and paid for, and they weren't cheap. Others – most of them – I've worked out for myself.

43

And they're not for sale. They're certainly not there to be stolen and *then* sold.'

The manager growled, 'You've a poor opinion of the profession, Gordon.'

Gordon said, 'I know human nature. I also know this show wouldn't fold if I left. But, equally, I know it would lose a good percentage of its pulling power. I'm part of the show. And if I'm to remain part of the show, I make my own rules as far as my own act is concerned. No qualifications. No arguments. Take it or leave it. Tell the others and tell them I don't give a damn about being popular. They know – *you* know – if I left the show today I'd be in another, probably better, show within a week.'

For a man so young to be so sure of himself. The manager was both angry and admiring, but being also a man well versed in the uncertainties of audience reaction he accepted the ultimatum without too much argument.

Then on a Sunday – when the show was 'resting' prior to the night journey to the next resort – Gordon telephoned for and received an appointment to visit David Devant.

Past his seventieth year, the great stage magician was failing; he still taught and wrote about magic; a hint of the charisma which had made him a household word in the early years of the century was still present, but it was plain to see that the casket to end all caskets would claim him within the next few years.

Over a quiet lunch they talked and, as was to be expected, their talk rarely drifted away from the giants of their own art.

'Chung Ling Soo.' Devant chuckled quietly. 'Bill Robinson . . . that was his real name. That was the first hurdle he had to overcome. He almost didn't make it . . . with a name like "Robinson". After his first try at solo he became stage manager and assistant to Harry Keller, then to Alex Herman. Then, when Herman died, he thought up the Mongolian idea.

Chung Ling Soo. A winner. A long act and he never spoke a word. I think – let me see? – yes, 1900 at the Alhambra, that was when he really caught the public's imagination. He was there all of three months. Never spoke a word. Pretended he didn't understand the English language. He used a stooge – a Korean actually – whenever he wanted the audience to know anything. A great showman. The whole of London – the whole of the United Kingdom *and* America – thought he *was* a Chinaman.'

'A legend,' murmured Gordon.

'For more than twenty years.' Devant nodded. 'Until he decided to include that damned bullet-catching trick.'

'Dangerous?' Gordon teased information and memories from the old wizard.

'Some tricks.' A sad, faraway look misted Devant's eyes. 'They should be outlawed. Good tricks, but they should be outlawed. If things go wrong, somebody gets hurt. Somebody gets killed. That bullet-catching routine. It had been done before. Fairly often. A pistol – a rifle – and the illusionist takes the bullet on a plate held in front of his chest. Catches the bullet on the plate. Standard three-o-three ammunition . . . that's what's used. The rifle's doctored obviously. It retains the bullet. But the problem . . . eh? To actually explode the bullet in the normal way, but at the same time allow the gases to escape and prevent the bullet from leaving the rifle. The strain on the necessary mechanism is very great. Sometimes too great. Chung Ling Soo wasn't the first illusionist killed by that trick. He won't be the last . . . whilever magicians perform that trick there'll be fatalities.'

Thus the talk. The master and the pupil. The once-great and the would-be-great. Gordon did most of the listening, but when Devant asked questions Gordon didn't hesitate to answer. It was quite safe; the closed freemasonry of stage magicians ensured that the secrets of Gordon's illusions would remain secret.

45

At last Devant said, 'Are you prepared to take advice?'

'Eager,' said Gordon. 'That's why I'm here.'

'I think . . .' The old man pondered his words carefully. 'I think you're as far as you're likely to get without an assistant.'

Gordon frowned.

'A good act – a complete act,' explained Devant, 'requires complete co-operation. Two people . . . at least two people.'

'You mean a double-act? Like Maskelyne and yourself?'

'Not necessarily. Or at least not *obviously*.' Devant rested his chin on the closed fist of his right hand, with the extended forefinger following the line of his jaw. He rested his elbow on the arm of his chair. He said, 'Before I joined Jasper's father, John Maskelyne had a principal assistant. Charles Morritt. Morritt was good enough to be an illusionist – a conjurer – in his own right, but he worked with John. I've already explained. Even Chung Ling Soo worked as assistant – first to Keller, then to Herman.

'John Maskelyne and I shared equal billing, but we each were the other's assistant. Indeed we had other assistants on stage with us when necessary. "The Maskelyne and Devant Mysteries". Before your time, of course, we opened in August 1905 at the St George's Hall. We continued for years. Some of our illusions became almost legendary. The Mascot Moth. The Artist's Dream. Fine illusions, though I say it myself. Never bettered. But no one man could have performed those illusions alone. A partner was needed. A fellow-magician . . . even if that fellow-magician masqueraded as a mere stage-help.

'You see, Mr Gordon, the art of illusion is the art of distraction. The audience must *think* it is watching all the time. But there must be one moment when the audience is *not* watching. Only a split second. But without that split second the illusion becomes impossible. No amount of mechanical trickery can replace that flicker of distraction, especially when a truly big illusion is being presented. The time of the distraction. The manner of the distraction. Each magician attends to these finer details personally. But for there to *be* the required distraction, there has to be a partner. A Number One Assistant. Somebody who knows as much about the trick, and the timing of the trick, as the man performing it.

'For example – and this has been done hundreds of times – the "clumsy" assistant. The assistant who disarrays a drape. Stumbles slightly on entrance. Drops some unimportant object.' Devant smiled. 'The audience – every audience, even the most appreciative – wants something to go wrong occasionally. Wants to spot a mistake. Accept that and you can *give* them the mistake they desire. A carefully contrived mistake. A different mistake each evening, a mistake rehearsed and perfected between your partner and yourself. Think, Mr Gordon. A magician's mind can come up with a hundred mock-mistakes. A never-ending supply. A slight collision on stage. The clumsy handling of a piece of equipment. An untied shoe threatening to leave the assistant's foot. And – always – the look of annoyance, the flash of anger, on the magician's face. Part of the illusion . . . surely? The great tricks – the tricks which have become a part of the history of stage magic – required the skill of two people . . . *always*.'

LONGER LOOK (PART ONE)

We look before and after;
We pine for what is not;
Our sincerest laughter
With some pain is fraught;
Our sweetest songs are those that tell
    of saddest thought.

To A Skylark
Percy Bysshe Shelley

One day an under-employed civil servant from some Ministry or another will tour the head,..rters of the United Kingdom police forces and compare each office occupied by chief constables, assistant chief constables, deputy chief constables and heads of C.I.D. It will be a boring task because he will see the same large, polished-topped desk, the same dark red, thin-piled carpet, the same glass-fronted cabinet displaying the same array of cups and plates won by various successful teams, the same leather-bottomed, swivel desk-chair, the same handful of high-backed chairs for the use of visitors . . . the same *everything*.

There is, it would seem, a peculiar lack of inventiveness when it comes to furnishing these offices; they are cheerless, dismal places. They smell of beeswax, pomposity and (sometimes) floral-scented air-freshener. They have an echoing remoteness from reality; a remoteness not far removed from that encountered in a funeral parlour or a chapel of rest.

Which perhaps is why most chief constables, assistant chief constables, deputy chief constables and heads of C.I.D. spend as little time as possible in their respective offices.

Pilter hated the place. On a normal day, he arrived at about nine-thirty, initialled or signed whatever documents required his initials or signature and was out of the place by noon. The afternoon he spent in the supervision of whatever major crimes the force was at that moment wrestling with, calling back at his own office at some time between five and six o'clock, as a salve to his own conscience and to make sure

51

nothing of paramount importance had happened during his absence.

Thus his daily routine.

But on the day following the death of George Gordon he broke that routine. Having arranged to meet Skeel there he arrived at his office at three o'clock in the afternoon. This time he wore what he privately called his 'fighting outfit'; brogue shoes, tweed trousers and jacket and – against the first bite of winter which rode the mid-November wind – a fleece-lined driving-coat.

'All fixed?' He asked the question as he shed the driving-coat and draped it over one of the high-backed chairs.

'Everything you asked for,' said Skeel. He smiled and added, 'Plus a bonus.'

'Later.' Pilter crossed to the desk. 'First we'll pull some teeth.' He lifted the telephone receiver from its rest and spoke into the mouthpiece. 'Chief Superintendent Pilter, here. The chief constable . . . can he spare me a few minutes?' There was a pause, then he said, 'Good. We'll be along. I have Detective Inspector Skeel with me.'

Pilter replaced the receiver and without pausing in his stride gave a soft and impatient snapping-finger gesture to Skeel, who hurried after him along the corridor and into the chief constable's office.

There was a silent dynamism about Pilter which had been absent the night before. It was as if *now* he was prepared to control the speed and direction of the enquiry; as if previously he had been content to allow it to roll forward without hindrance, with himself as an interested onlooker.

The chief constable watched the two men as they crossed the carpet to his desk. Once he'd been a good policeman – a renowned thief-taker – but today he showed the shiny signs of soft living; the gloss of too much lionisation; the paunch of inactivity and good food.

He beetled his heavy eyebrows and said, 'Pilter?'

'The Gordon death.' Pilter gave the impression that time was too precious to waste on unnecessary words.

'Ah, yes. I saw the report when I came in. Suspected murder.'

'*Possible* murder,' corrected Pilter.

'You're handling it personally?'

'Yes.'

'Good.'

'There's a character called Baxter.'

'Baxter?'

'Neil Baxter. He claims to be a friend of yours.'

'Oh . . . *that* Baxter.'

'Is he?' asked Pilter, bluntly.

'What?'

'A friend of yours?'

'What difference does it make?' The chief constable scowled.

'That,' said Pilter, 'is what I'm here to find out.'

'If he's the man you're after . . .'

'He's one of six.'

'Mr Pilter.' The chief constable's face reddened. 'The implication behind your words is offensive.'

'Good.' Pilter grinned. 'I had to make sure.'

'Was it necessary?' growled the chief constable.

'A possibility in this day and age.'

'Good God, man! I think I deserve . . .'

'No, sir.' Pilter's grin eased itself into a smile; a hard, tight smile of no compromise. 'No apology. At your best you'd have done the same. And like me you'd have brought a ranking officer along as witness.'

Back in Pilter's office Skeel said, 'My God, you chanced your arm there.'

'Not really,' murmured Pilter.

'If he *had* been a friend of Baxter . . .'

53

'It doesn't matter a damn either way now.'

'But if he *had* been a friend . . .'

'He's not now,' sighed Pilter. 'He *daren't* be. Spiking guns – pulling teeth – dammit, Skeel, you're a detective inspector, surely to hell you've learned by now to protect your own back by this time.'

Skeel blinked. For a moment – for perhaps the sliver of a second – he thought of raising some slight protest against Pilter's near-open contempt. Then he decided against. Pilter, as Skeel knew, was no respecter of persons; men – men holding rank as high as that held by Skeel – had been dumped on their backsides before now for crossing swords with Pilter. Skeel was, above all else, a disciple of self-preservation.

He swallowed his annoyance and said, 'I was – er – going to tell you.'

'When?'

'Before we went to the chief's office.'

'What?'

'Potassium cyanide. The post mortem this morning verifies it.'

'Good.'

'And we've found traces.' Skeel smiled his small triumph.

'In his guts?'

'In an empty condom packet.'

'In a . . .' Pilter froze as he threaded an arm through the driving-coat. He stared. 'In a *what*?'

'When we searched them last night. Baxter. We found the empty packet in the top pocket of his jacket. The breast-pocket behind his handkerchief. The lab telephoned just before you arrived. Traces of potassium powder.'

'In the French letter packet?'

Skeel nodded.

'Now,' said Pilter, 'I've heard everything.' He jerked the driving-coat into position across his shoulders. 'Get onto the

54

vice boys. Ask 'em. Is there something new in the kink line? Something we haven't heard about yet?'

'I hardly think . . .' began Skeel.

'Check.' Pilter buttoned his coat. 'Glue-sniffing. A few years back who'd have thought lunatics would have become addicted to the stench of glue? Potassium cyanide. Who knows, the silly buggers might have found a new use for it.'

'I'll – er – check.' Skeel sounded disappointed. He said, 'The *au pair* nurse. She'll be there, I had a word with her before I left last night. By the way, her name's Hulda Deschin.'

'Fine.' Pilter made for the door. 'Join us at the Castle Restaurant when you've had a word with the vice crowd.'

Pilter walked the mile or so to the Castle Restaurant because he needed the exercise and because he needed the air. A lifetime of sleep-at-all-hours-eat-when-you-can-fit-it-in existence had made him constitutionally immune from the normal hangdog feeling which for most men would have followed a session ending with the dawn poking cold fingers through the windows as he climbed into bed. But he needed extra fortification before another stint of working alongside Skeel.

Skeel brought out the worst in him. Skeel tended to stir a naturally blunt manner until it became almost uncouth. Skeel seemed to squat there on his shoulder like a sententious little elf, everlastingly reminding him of the thousand-and-one rules and regulations thought up by screaming maniacs who couldn't detect their way from a football ground. Skeel got on his bloody wick.

And yet . . .

The fact remained that in his own, narrow-minded way Skeel wasn't a bad copper. He couldn't be licked at the fiddling work, and the fiddling work more often than not brought home the bacon. Detection – be it murder or the nicking of milk bottles – had sod-all to do with magnifying glasses and deerstalker hats. Equally it had sod-all to do with sudden and blinding inspiration. Detection had *everything* to do with rooting away in the muck, like a pig nuzzling its way into swill. And with luck – and if the stench didn't overpower you first – the odd pearl ended up in your teeth. Enough pearls and you had a necklace . . . and you could chalk 'Detected' across one more crime.

And (fair licks) Skeel had a knack of groping around and finding pearls other men might have missed. A knack. Something he was capable of. A knack he'd been born with. But without flair. Like last night. The adjutant when he should have been the C.O. Not *quite* in command, when by Christ he *should* have been.

Damnation, Gordon's death was as simple as a seven-piece jigsaw puzzle. Kid's stuff. Seven people – Gordon, his wife, Baxter, Baxter's wife, Hector, Dobson and Dearden – and one of them *had* to have slipped the cyanide into the rum-and-pep. If Gordon, it was suicide. If anybody else, it was murder. Bloody hell, they didn't *come* any more simple than that. No house-to-house time-wasting. No questionnaire rubbish. No search. No nothing.

And yet there he'd been, farting around screaming for moral support. He'd wanted a search. A personal search, a body-search, and he'd lacked the simple guts to go ahead and organise one.

And why?

Because Baxter 'knew' the chief constable. Judas Christ! A detective inspector and he hadn't yet realised that when the splinters started pricking their arse, everybody on God's earth 'knew' somebody. It was the oldest fairy story ever told. It had whiskers on it. And Skeel still sucked.

Pilter muttered, 'Sod him,' shoved his hands deeper into the pockets of his coat and lengthened his stride.

The Castle Restaurant. Why the Castle Restaurant? Well,

56

because it had to be called *something*. There wasn't a castle or even a castellated building within twenty miles. The place itself didn't look like a castle. Nor had anybody called Castle ever been the proprietor of the place. It was just the Castle Restaurant ... take it or leave it.

It specialised in what the more snooty-nosed Victorians called High Tea. Fancy cakes oozing real cream. Gateaux. Chocolate éclairs. Truffles. And, of course, pots of tea to be sipped from doll's-house-sized teacups.

The woman, Hulda Deschin, was seated at a table within the bow of the mock-Georgian window. She was alone and the only other occupants of the restaurant were an elderly couple with their over-fat, cross-bred terrier sprawling, suspicious-eyed, by the man's feet. Therefore the solitary woman had to be Hulda Deschin.

She was a little older than Pilter had expected; the expression *'au pair'* had dolly-bird connotations and Hulda Deschin was, at a guess, in her early thirties. She was squatter than he'd expected; heavier built than he'd expected; and she wore a somewhat severe two-piece outfit with a high-necked blouse. There was about her a certain seriousness – a certain sombre-eyed tranquillity – which (or so it seemed to Pilter) had a distinctive Germanic quality about it.

He walked to the table and said, 'Miss Deschin?'

'Ah!' She smiled; a quick on-and-off movement of the lips. 'Mr Pilter.'

'May I?' Pilter touched one of the empty chairs.

'Please. Sit down.'

The waitress arrived at the table and Pilter ordered tea and a choice of cakes. They chatted gratuitous conversation, until their order was placed on the table and the waitress retired out of earshot.

Then as he spooned sugar into his tea Pilter said, 'The Gordons, Miss Deschin.'

57

She waited. Silently. A look of mild puzzlement in her eyes.

'Would he have committed suicide?' he asked gently.

'It is possible.'

'He was that type?'

'I'm sorry?'

'That type? The sort of person who might commit suicide?'

'Could not you, Mr Pilter?' She in turn moved the spoon in her tea in order to dissolve the sugar. 'Any of us? Could not any of us take our life?'

'Okay.' He nodded brief acknowledgement of the proposition. 'That being the case why should George Gordon commit suicide?'

She moved her shoulders.

'There has to be a reason,' insisted Pilter.

'They have their reasons. People have reasons for these things.'

'Agreed, but what was Gordon's reason?'

She hesitated, then said, 'He was not a happy man.'

'The wheelchair?'

'That also.'

'And what else?'

'He had . . . what is it?' She sought the right word. 'Frustration?'

'Frustrated.'

'He was frustrated.' She nodded. 'He worked great magic once. Before great audiences. Here. In America. In Europe. On the stage he performed the impossible. Men said there had been none like him. None as great. No trickery as great as his trickery.'

'Trickery?' Pilter frowned.

'The Great Gordano,' she murmured.

'Christ!'

'You didn't know?' She smiled.

'No.' Pilter sipped at his tea. 'No, I didn't know. I – er –

'I saw him once. Just the once. Years ago, I was in my teens at the time. London. A bit of a holiday. The Prince of Wales Theatre. The whole show. The sort of show you never forget.'

'The Great Gordano,' she said gently.

'I didn't know,' muttered Pilter. 'I thought he'd retired, y'know . . . retired.'

'My father worked with him,' she said.

'Your father?'

'He, too, was a magician. A fine magician. He worked with Gordano.'

'So that's why . . .' Pilter raised his eyebrows.

'I was a nurse. Mr Gordon required a nurse. I wished to improve my English. It seemed sensible.'

'Quite.' Pilter linked his fingers and rested his forearms on the table. For a moment he seemed to be recovering from the shock of knowing the identity of the dead man. Then he said, 'You knew him then? I mean, you've known him for a long time? Knew him for a long time? Not just as a nurse?'

'Since I was a schoolgirl.'

'What sort of man was he?'

'Gordano?'

'Gordano. George Gordon. What sort of a *man* was he?'

To be the last of the great illusionists. To be the ultimate of what was born in the mists of pre-recorded history; to have unravelled the secrets of ancient Indian and Persian magicians; to have trained the mind to a point where the word 'impossible' is viewed as merely one more problem to be solved.

To be The Great Gordano.

The priest-magicians of old were strange men. Their power was limitless. They could perform 'miracles', therefore they were feared by kings and monarchs. They were a class unto themselves. Isolated from all other men. This being the case they became creatures of legend . . . and because of what they were they encouraged such legends. They secreted themselves behind battlements of involved ritual. They were worshipped as gods, or at the very least as companions of gods. The elements were their playthings. The winds were theirs to command, the rain was theirs to control, the sun and moon were their friends and all natural catastrophes occurred only at their bidding.

Such power, or to be accurate such supposed-power, was – always had been, always would be – a base-line for a peculiar madness. To be able seemingly to defy the laws of nature is a small step short of the belief that those laws can in fact be defied. Magicians, tricksters, illusionists . . . more than a few have dabbled in the so-called Black Art. Witchcraft to them has seemed little more than a logical progression from their own craft.

George Gordon?

No man knew more than he about the history of his profession. No man was more appreciative of the pitfalls and the temptations, after all, hadn't Harry Houdini himself dabbled in the occult? To be a stage magician was one thing, but to be a practitioner in the pseudo-art of 'true' magic was another. Nevertheless, and because of his own fanaticism concerning legerdemain, Gordon was curious. The two arts – the art of deception and the Black Art – were near-companions; indeed, accept that the Black Art was a fiction, and they were the same thing. Both were deliberate frauds.

And yet . . .

Once, in a pensive mood, he remarked, 'This thing the theatrical profession have about *Macbeth*. The name of the play must not be mentioned while it is being performed in a theatre. Actors, actresses who are happy to take on any other Shakespearean role seek some excuse when asked to perform in that particular play. It's more than coincidence. It has to be more than coincidence. The catalogue of misfortune attached to the production of that play – the proven and indisputable catalogue of misfortune – makes coincidence an absurdity.

'Witchcraft. The so-called Ancient Religion. The sixteenth and seventeenth centuries . . . one of the great periods of witch-cult. I must give credence to the theory. That Shakespeare knew more about witchcraft than he might have admitted. That the opening scene in *Macbeth* – the witches' scene – includes genuine incantations. A black joke. The sort of joke played by a man of Shakespeare's temperament. An insolent genius. A man prepared to damn his own work as a means of showing the extent of his own knowledge.

'But you see, accept that and you must accept the validity of the incantations. The validity of witchcraft. The validity of at least some form of genuine magic. However much mumbo-jumbo involved a percentage of it must be true. And if a percentage, how big a percentage?'

'He believed in it then?'

'The witch-cult? Black magic?' Hulda Deschin re-filled her cup from the teapot.

'From what you say,' said Pilter, 'he believed, or at least half-believed, in the supernatural. The supernormal.'

'I think.' She nodded solemnly. She added, 'I think all magicians – stage magicians – think so. I think they must believe if they are to perform their tricks with assurance.'

'So . . .' Pilter rubbed his jaw meditatively. 'A man with a high opinion of himself.'

'Of course.'

'Who believed – possibly believed – the magic he performed on stage might also be performed without trickery.'

'No.' She shook her head. 'That is too simple, Mr Pilter. To vanish a lion from its cage – one of his conjurings – that is impossible without trickery. No, the more gentle things.

61

The more frightening things. These, I think, he believed in.'

'Such as?'

'Hypnotism. Tht great mystery, the Indian Rope Trick. My father once explained it. It cannot be performed. Never! It must merely *seem* to be performed. The audience must be made to believe that they have seen what they have *not* seen.'

'Mass hypnotism?'

'The only way.' She smiled gently. 'Mr Pilter. You are a policeman. Your life – the things you take for granted – they would surprise and shock me perhaps. The world of the stage. The world of magic. I was born into it. It, too, is a strange world. That trick – the Indian Rope Trick – it is impossible. Believe me. It is impossible. To throw a rope into the air; to make it stand upright; to allow a boy to climb that rope and, at the top of that rope, vanish. To perform that trick in the open. In a market place without trickery. Where trickery cannot be. Impossible! And yet . . .' Again she smiled. 'I know men and women who will swear they have seen the trick performed. *Swear*. Good people. Honest people. They have seen it, but they have not. They only *think* they have seen it.'

'And Gordon?'

'A trick he wished to perform.' There was a sighing quality about the words.

'Hypnotising a whole audience?' Disbelief was there. Disbelief almost amounting to scorn.

'I think.' She held her head slightly to one side, as if pondering upon her next words before speaking them. She said, 'Yes . . . I think he could have performed that trick, too.'

Pilter was suddenly aware of somebody standing at his shoulder.

Skeel said, 'Can I have a word with you?'

'Yes.'

'In private.'

62

Pilter pursed his lips, murmured, 'Excuse me for a minute,' pushed back his chair, then followed Skeel to the entrance alcove of the restaurant.

'Something kinky?' he asked.

'What?' Skeel looked puzzled.

'The cyanide? Have the vice boys come up with . . .'

'Oh . . . *that*?' Understanding dawned on Skeel's face. 'No, not that. The pathologist. He's been busy most of the day. Meant to telephone you as soon as possible. But . . .'

'Don't tell me it's not cyanide poisoning.'

'No, not that. But, y'know, the legs. The wheelchair was unnecessary.'

'Come again.' Pilter stared.

'He could walk. That's the opinion of the pathologist. That wheelchair. It was a put-on.'

'Why the hell should a man want to . . .'

'That's what the pathologist thought.' Skeel fumbled a used envelope from an inside pocket. 'I have the pathologist's home telephone number. In case you'd like a word.'

'I'd like a word.' Pilter still looked a little dazed. 'I'd like a few words. With him. With a lot of people . . . including the fräulein guzzling tea.'

'Incontinent,' said Pilter. The façade of polite conversation was missing. The word – the tone – held a cool harshness. He stared at the woman and said, 'His bowels. His bladder. Could he control 'em?'

'Er – er – *das badezimmer*. Er – *die toilette*.' Skeel moved his hands and flicked his fingers as he struggled with school-boy German. '*Allein*. Y'know . . . *allein*.'

'Of course. Why not?' The woman looked startled.

'Why not what?' snapped Pilter.

'Why not use the toilet – the bathroom – alone? Only his legs were paralysed. The rest of him was . . . normal.'

'Normal?'

'But of course.'

'But not his legs?'

'His legs were without feeling. Nothing.'

Pilter glanced at Skeel and Skeel looked well out of his depth.

'You doubt this?' She wrinkled her forehead in puzzlement as she asked the question.

'Let's say I need convincing,' growled Pilter. 'Now the bathroom, the toilet . . . who helped him?'

'Nobody.'

'Not even you?'

'No. He was a proud man.'

'If he'd no use in his legs, he'd need a bloody sight more than pride. He'd need . . .'

'He had rails.'

'Ah!'

'Bars. An arrangement. He could pull himself into the bath. Onto the toilet. Into bed. He demanded privacy.'

'No help from anybody?'

'Nobody.'

'His wife?'

'Nobody,' she repeated. 'At night he would ring and I would collect his clothes. Arrange new clothes for morning.'

'After he was in bed?'

She nodded.

Skeel cleared his throat and said, 'What were *your* functions, miss?'

'I'm sorry?' Her expression showed non-understanding.

'As a nurse,' amplified Pilter. 'What were your duties?'

'He was a sick man. A cripple.'

'Fine, but what did you *do*? Specifically?'

'I wheeled him from room to room. To the lift. If he . . .'

'He used a lift?'

'To get downstairs. To get upstairs. Of course.'

'And that's all?'

64

'I'm sorry?'

'Just pushing the wheelchair around? That's all you did?'

'When he was ill, I . . .'

'Was he ill often?'

'No.' She frowned as if at a sudden realisation. 'He was a strong man. He had great pride. He . . .'

'You keep stressing that,' said Pilter.

'What?'

'The "pride" bit. If he was so infernally proud, why not have a mechanical wheelchair?'

She shook her head. The impression was that she was being made to view things in a new light. It was there in the slight frown of worry – of incomprehension – which remained part of her expression.

'The – er – sleeping pills.' She made it sound almost like an apology.

'He took sleeping pills?' said Pilter.

'Each night. When I went for his clothes, I gave him the pills with a glass of water.'

'Big deal,' murmured Pilter. 'You must have been rushed off your feet.'

'I'm – er . . .'

'I know . . . you're sorry.'

'Who was his doctor?' asked Skeel.

'Dr Austin.'

Pilter said, 'You worked under *his* instructions. Right?'

'I – I suppose.' She hesitated, then added, 'There was little to do. I see that now. Little to do. I telephoned Dr Austin when new sleeping pills were needed. Other than that . . . very little.'

They rode back to the police station in Skeel's car. Skeel drove while Pilter stared ahead and for the first time wondered whether this *was* one of those tortuous, mind-blowing bastards which, just occasionally, drive hard-working coppers up the nearest wall.

Potassium cyanide. Not one of these fancy, mysterious poisons. Any damn fool with a bit of gumption could lay his hands on potassium cyanide. Tons of the bloody stuff lying around without real security. Industry – especially the various branches of the chemical industry – used the stuff by the bucketful. No problem. 'You have some spare potassium cyanide, mate?' 'Sure, how much do you want?' As easy as *that*. So trotting round the various chemist shops and checking the poison registers was likely to be an almighty waste of time.

Something to keep Skeel out of his hair.

He muttered, 'The usual rigmarole, inspector.'

'What?' Skeel kept his eyes on the road ahead.

'Poison registers.'

'Oh!'

'Check on who's bought potassium cyanide, say during the last year.'

Skeel sighed, but accepted the drudgery without complaint.

Pilter wondered why the hell Skeel never snapped back; why the man was a walking doormat. Maybe that was why he (Pilter) didn't like him too much. Why he was a perpetual pain in the neck. One mistake – just one juicy clanger – it might make him more human. Might make him more popular. A bit like a wheelbarrow. All you had to do was load him up, point him and push . . . and away he went. As unimaginative as a bloody wheelbarrow.

Screw Skeel!

This blasted nurse, though, this Hulda Deschin woman, she was one of two things. As thick as two short planks or bloody crafty. A nurse and all she did was push a wheelchair around and, when necessary, shake sleeping pills out of a box. Some nurse! Now if *she'd* been around when Gordon swallowed the poison . . .

HULDA DESCHIN

Berlin, 1953. Something approaching normality – 'Berlin normality' – had returned. The Airlift of '48/'49 was a thing of recent memory; a memory not fully understood and not fully appreciated by a five-year-old child. And yet, she already knew the meaning of fear.

Not fear of the dark. Not fear of giants or bogey-men. Not the fears experienced by other non-German children of her age; fears which are part of growing up; fears which are little more than excitements with which to spice a world mainly of make-believe.

Hers was a real fear, but a fear she could not understand.

So many non-Germans in the streets. Americans, Britishers, French and – worst of all – Russians. So many non-Germans, and so much ill-concealed contempt. Contempt which amounted to a silent, glowering hatred.

There had been a war. Evidence of the war was there to see; the mountains of rubble which still flanked so many streets; the air of sadness and despair worn by so many grown-ups. There had been a war. There had been a leader. A man called Hitler; a saviour or a devil; a genius or a madman. She didn't know which. Some adults said one thing, some adults said the other. But undoubtedly there had been a leader called Adolph Hitler. There had been Nazis. What were Nazis? She didn't know. To her it was a meaningless word. No! Not a meaningless word. A word, but a word with meaning; a word which triggered off this terrifying – this unreasonable – hatred. Therefore a word with meaning.

Her mother was dead. She couldn't even remember her mother. The manner of her death was a secret thing; not discussed; not even spoken of. That it had something to do with this pointless hatred . . . this she knew, but it was a knowledge acquired via a child's sharpened sense of aware-

67

ness, as nobody had ever explained the circumstances of that death to her.

Her father?

Once a soldier. Once part of the Afrika Korps. Then, after a bullet in one of his lungs, a civilian. An official in the Berlin Air Protection Service; a junior official, working within the local branch of the German Economic Ministry; a clerk – little more than a clerk – at the local Supply Office and supervising the issue of coupons for the necessities of life after an air attack.

A Nazi?

He was a German. That was enough for five-year-old Hulda Deschin. A German and a good father – a man who at that time was touting his talents as a conjurer around the nightspots which were springing up around the punch-drunk city . . . that was enough for Hulda Deschin.

He was a German.

That, too, was enough for those hate-filled foreigners. He was a German – therefore he was ex-Nazi; and Hulda was his daughter.

The Rover's headlights cleared a path of visibility through the early evening darkness. Already the dying verge-grass glistened with the first touch of night-frost; beyond the grass the irregularly spaced trees which punctuated the hedgerows looked gnarled and naked – like unclothed and deformed women – without their splendour of leaf.

Ahead of him lay Baxter and questions.

Behind him he'd left a pathologist, and some answers which in turn had spawned other questions.

'Those lower limbs – those lower muscles – the calf, the thigh, the foot – they're undamaged. The nervous system is complete. There's no reason on earth why the man should have been confined to a wheelchair.'

'You're sure of that?'

'Chief superintendent, I know my job.'

'Granted, but . . .'

'The man could walk. Run if necessary. What's more he *has* walked – or at the very least used his legs vigorously and recently. The muscles – the nerves – the tendons . . . they're all in tip-top condition. An athlete wouldn't be ashamed of such legs.'

'You'll – er – you'll give that evidence at the inquest?'

'If I'm asked, I'll give that evidence. That's how sure I am.'

Which was very cosy if you happened to be a pathologist, but one hell of a kick in the teeth if you happened to be a hard-working copper.

People did crazy things. Okay, they did crazy things. They poured petrol all over themselves and struck matches. They shinned all the way up Nelson's Column. They leaped railway-cuttings on motor bikes. And always they had a reason, to try to *prove* something. But what in hell's name could a man prove by keeping his arse anchored to an invalid's chair for the rest of his life? Why the big play-act? Why deny that he could walk? And if he *had* to deny that he could walk, why keep his walking muscles in trim?

Pilter blew out his cheeks in disgust, and turned his mind to broader generalities.

Himself . . .

Policing . . .

Time was (when he'd first bought himself a police number) when being a bobby *meant* something. When the end of a war had spewed men from the armed forces and almost overnight the Police Service had undergone a change. Coppers with every medal ribbon under the sun stitched to the front of their tunics. Men with a built-in discipline, tailor-made for another war . . . a war against crime. Men who'd been taught how to fight; how to guard each other's backs; how to be top-dog in any situation. Those had been the days. Great days! For those first few years – ten years or thereabouts – the bent bastards hadn't known Sunday from Pancake Tuesday. They'd been knocked dizzy. They'd crawled back into their knot-holes and for the first time – for the first time forever – the lice had *not* ruled the world.

Great days!

Today? A handful left . . . no more than a handful. Top-rankers, like himself. Those who hadn't made rank had had sense enough to walk away and draw a pension. And why not? The lice had made a come-back in a big way. The lice and the sons of lice. You name it, friend, and there was a fiddle attached. A 'Mister Fix-it' somewhere in the background.

That and too many men like Skeel. How in hell could a police force function with nerks like Skeel gumming up the machinery? Soppy bastards who hadn't the guts to lead with a left when things started being hairy. Civil liberties fodder; pansy-minded she-men who couldn't bring themselves to slap the germs into a dock each way and any way and screw what the fairies-at-the-bottom-of-the-garden lunatics screamed.

What was it? . . . a community gets the police it deserves. Too damned true. It also gets the crooks it deserves; the vandals it deserves; the hooligans it deserves; the crime-wave it deserves. And, friend, that made this a very sick society.

Maybe *that* was why Gordon loved his wheelchair.

Maybe it was his way of opting out.

Baxter wasn't pleased and in his present mood Pilter couldn't care less about Baxter's annoyance.

As Baxter led the detective chief superintendent into the lounge of the expensively modernised farmhouse he grumbled, 'I must admit that this is an inconvenient time, Pilter.'

'Yeah, for me, too,' growled Pilter. 'Life works that way sometimes.'

'I thought last night . . .'

'Last night was the overture. This is the first act.'

'I see you're alone.'

'You, too.'

'My wife's staying with her sister . . . until after the funeral.'

'Mrs Gordon?'

'My sister-in-law. I thought you knew?'

'Officially I haven't been told.'

'But now?'

'Now I know . . . officially.'

That first conversational pat-ball set the pace; each mistrusted the other and nobody was going to give an inch. Baxter fancied himself. He was nobody's mug and men were still struggling to their feet . . . men who'd thought otherwise. Nevertheless, it was no contest. Baxter was only a skilled amateur. Pilter was a professional Grand Master.

Baxter waved the detective chief superintendent towards the opulence of one of the overtly expensive armchairs, smiled and said, 'You're on duty. I won't offer you a drink.'

'They only refuse in detective stories.' Pilter returned the smile.

'In that case?' Baxter raised his eyebrows.

'Whisky with soda. Not too much soda.'

'Double?'

'Or triple . . . it's your whisky.'

'You really *are* different.' Baxter's smile became slightly fixed.

'Among friends.'

Baxter fixed the drinks, while Pilter settled himself more comfortably into the cushionwork. Neither of them spoke until Baxter had handed Pilter the drink, prior to him flopping down into one of the companion armchairs.

Then Baxter said, 'Well?'

Pilter moistened his lips, nodded appreciatively and murmured, 'Nice whisky.' He held it high enough for the light

71

from a stand-lamp to send an added glow through the golden liquid, then said, '*Very* nice whisky.'

'Presumably, you didn't come all this way out to . . .'

'Assuming it contained potassium cyanide. Where from?'

'Eh?'

'The potassium cyanide. Where would you have got it from?'

'What the devil do *I* want with potassium cyanide?'

'You tell me.' Pilter lowered the glass and smiled.

'I don't even know what potassium cyanide looks . . .'

'A white, crystalline powder. A bit like sugar.'

'Really. Well – I'm sorry – but I'm an accountant, not a . . .'

'A partner in this agency thing.'

'The Gordon Agency. Yes, I'm . . .'

'And a farmer.'

'Obviously. You're here at . . .'

'And farmers use potassium cyanide sometimes. Vermin control . . . that sort of thing.'

'Do they?'

'Didn't you know?' Pilter put exactly the right weight of mild surprise into the question.

'The farm's more of a hobby,' growled Baxter.

'An expensive hobby.'

'It helps beat the tax man.'

'I'm sure.'

'And I've a man – an agent – who runs the place.'

'Everybody an agent.' Pilter sipped the whisky.

'It's a word,' said Baxter sardonically.

'Of course. Like "farmer". Like "suicide".'

Baxter's eyes narrowed slightly as he said, 'You think *not* suicide?'

'I think . . .' Pilter moistened his lips with the whisky. 'I think – when I'm *allowed* to think – when I have *time* to think . . . I think most people are capable of murder.'

'That George was murdered?'

'George?'

'Gordon.'

'Ah! The Great Gordano.'

'It wasn't a secret,' said Baxter.

'That he was murdered?' asked Pilter innocently.

'That he was The Great Gordano.'

'No, but it wasn't public knowledge.'

'We all have different lives,' observed Baxter.

'Of course, until somebody slips cyanide into our rum-and-pep.'

Baxter chuckled and said, 'You've a one-track mind, Pilter.'

'At the moment.'

'Well . . .' Baxter enjoyed a mouthful of whisky. '*I* didn't kill him.'

'You'd be surprised.' This time Pilter chuckled.

'What?'

'The chances are Cain said that when he'd clobbered Abel.'

'That's almost an accusation, superintendent.' Again the eyes narrowed.

'Think so?'

'As I mentioned last night . . .'

'I know. You're a friend of the chief.'

'I don't like reminding you of the fact.'

'Not any more, Baxter.' The tone was mild. The smile was mocking.

'What?'

Pilter drawled, 'End of a glorious friendship . . . you were *once* his friend. Maybe.'

'What the hell . . .'

'The expression is known as "closing ranks".'

'Since when . . .'

'Since we found traces of potassium cyanide in an empty French letter packet.'

Baxter stared.

'In the top pocket of *your* jacket. Last night. Since then – sorry, the chief constable can't even spell your name.'

'You're – you're crazy.' Baxter threw whisky down his throat.

'I'm open to certification,' said Pilter reasonably.

'That bloody packet. You don't think *I* put the damn thing there.'

'Unless you hire your top pocket out as a waste disposal unit.'

'For Christ's sake, I don't use the damn things.'

'Who knows? You may have old-fashioned tastes.'

'I've never used a condom in my life.'

Pilter smiled.

'You don't believe me,' rasped Baxter.

Pilter said, 'How the hell do I know? I don't check whether or not you're improperly dressed every time you get on the nest.'

Baxter breathed, 'You're a foul bastard, Pilter.'

'I know. Make the most of it. There's few of us left.'

'You're – you're insult-proof.'

'Naturally. It goes with the job.' Pilter leaned forward and placed his glass carefully on the carpet near his feet. As he straightened he said, 'Okay, Baxter, you've had your head of steam. Now it's my turn. Gordon died. Cyanide poisoning. Cyanide in his rum-and-pep. Gordon's anchored to a wheel-chair. The rest of you – you in particular – are floating around, helping yourselves to booze and what have you. Passing Gordon's chair. Passing the table and the rum-and-pep. The knock-out powder was slipped into the glass on the table. Everybody's searched. In the top pocket of your jacket we find an empty condom packet. In the folds of that packet we find traces of potassium cyanide. Now, take your time, you tell me . . . how many people do *you* think might have been hawking potassium cyanide around last night?'

'That's ridiculous.' The words had a groaning quality. A quality of defeat. They went with the paled face and the look of fear in the eyes.

'Take your time,' soothed Pilter.

'I didn't kill him . . . I swear!'

'But you'd cause.'

'P-perhaps.'

Thus the skill of a good detective; in three words, phrased not as a question, but as a pseudo-statement of fact . . . and the reaction. To read a man's face – to read a man's tone of voice . . . then to make a calculated guess. Pilter had done it too many times before. The near-admission was all he'd been angling for.

'Motive,' he murmured.

'Hell, that's no motive . . . no motive at all. Not for *murder*.'

'You'd be surprised.'

'For God's sake! You don't think . . .'

'I haven't heard your side of it, yet.'

NEIL BAXTER (2)

Actually, it was Gordon's idea. A good idea. 1976. The Great Gordano was finished; big magical acts had had their day and already Gordon had come to terms with the invalid chair.

But in the first place Gordon's idea.

'Neil, I have this scheme. There's room for an agency. A good agency.'

'An agency? What sort of an agency?'

'Theatrical. The northern club circuit. They're hungry for acts . . . good acts. I know. I have the contacts. They have the money. They pay more money than the old-timers ever knew existed. And they're hungry for good acts.'

75

'Sure, but where are the good acts who don't yet have agents?'

'The semi-pro crowd, Neil. The pickings are good. I know talent when I see it. I'll audition. All I need is somebody capable of taking care of the cash side of things. Somebody to visit the concert secretaries. My name still means something. My guarantee carries weight. Good acts. Polished acts. I'll find them. You sell them. They all want to turn pro. I'll make them professionals. I'll show them how. They'll sell their souls . . . their souls! Find a good solicitor. I want a contract. Air-tight, water-tight, bomb-proof. They'll sign. All you have to do is sell.'

Gordon's idea . . . all the way.

A good idea, too. The concert secretaries were eager and waiting. No sweat. And gradually a second, a subsidiary, money-maker became apparent. Stag Night acts. Strippers . . . plus. Flesh flicks. The Gordon Agency didn't handle such merchandise. Not the agency, but why not one part of that agency?

Hard cash, of course. No tooling around with cheques. Nothing that might have to go through banks or books. But enough folding stuff and anything. Anything!

And, why not, for Christ's sake? Young Turks – old rams – they want the old tits-arse-and-fanny show for real or on film . . . their morals were their own affair. That was where the money was and money was the name of the game.

'Unknown to Gordon of course,' observed Pilter.

In a low voice Baxter said, 'He'd have had my guts.'

'He might have found out,' suggested Pilter.

'How the hell could he have found out. It never went through . . .'

'People talk.'

'Not about things like that.'

'If he *had* found out,' mused Pilter.

76

'No way.' But there was a hint of uncertainty in the words.

'I found out,' smiled Pilter.

'How the hell, I'll never know.'

'People talk,' repeated Pilter. 'Sometimes the most unlikely people.'

'He didn't know.' But now the uncertainty was marginally greater.

'The agency,' said Pilter. 'What was the split between you?'

'Sixty-forty.'

'You took the forty?'

Baxter nodded.

'This place?' Pilter raised an eyebrow. 'Lush. And how many acres?'

'A hundred-and-eighty . . . about.'

'Pedigree stock?'

Baxter nodded.

'On forty-per-cent? And he didn't know? Couldn't *guess*?'

'He's never seen the place.'

'His wife?'

'She – er . . .' Baxter moistened his lips. 'She wouldn't tell him.'

'No?'

'She wouldn't tell him,' repeated Baxter.

'Wives do . . . sometimes,' said Pilter, gently.

'Not Ruth.' Baxter hesitated, then added, 'We were having this . . . thing.'

'Thing?'

'Y'know . . . an affair.'

'You really do live dangerously, Baxter.'

Baxter managed to smile as he said, 'Women find me attractive.'

'With a broken neck?' countered Pilter drily. He finished his whisky then said, 'Re-fills. It's a long time since I tasted expensive booze . . . and *you're* going to need one.'

The last half-dozen words wiped the smile from Baxter's face. He pushed himself from the armchair, collected Pilter's glass and mixed more whisky and soda.

When Baxter was once more seated, Pilter continued speaking. His tone was conversational. Almost lazy; much as the steel-springed stroll of a big cat is 'lazy' when the prey is cornered and helpless.

'Facts,' he drawled. 'Facts first. Gordon is dead, whether or not he's gone to glory is a matter of some debate. But sure as hell he's dead. Equally certain is the fact that he died suddenly from an excess of potassium cyanide. You were with him at the time. Others too, granted, but for the moment we'll concentrate on *you*. You – along with the others – were searched. And – Presto!, as The Great Gordano might have put it – one empty condom packet with traces of potassium cyanide found in the breast pocket of your jacket.'

Pilter held up a hand to silence Baxter as he continued, 'That's what's known as "concrete evidence" in the world of lawyers. They also have another fancy expression. *Res gestae.* Facts surrounding a case. Relevancies. Coppers, being coppers, tend to have simple minds as far as *res gestae*'s concerned. They call it "motive" . . . and leave it at that. So let's have a quick shufty at possible motive. *Your* possible motive.

'A hypothetical situation. You're charged with the murder of Gordon. You . . . personally. The "concrete evidence"? I've already itemised it. The *res gestae*? You're a farmer. Farmers have use for potassium cyanide. More *res gestae* – let's call it "motive" this time – you've been twisting Gordon bald and you've been shacking up with his wife. A small assumption that Gordon knew. And knowing he was on the point of crucifying you. You're with me, so far? Okay . . . enter self-preservation. Cyanide in Gordon's drink.' Pilter paused to sip whisky, then ended, 'Baxter, I could lift you here and now, and the boy paid to defend you wouldn't sleep nights.'

'You'd have to prove Gordon knew.' Baxter's voice might have been that of a man fighting for his life.

'True.' Pilter nodded.

'You'd have to prove somebody told him these things.'

'He could, y'know,' murmured Pilter.

'Yeah, but *he* was fixed to a wheelchair.'

'And if he hadn't been?'

'Then I might worry.'

'He still had ears,' said Pilter gently.

'Nobody told him.' The tone wasn't as certain as the words.

'No?'

'Nobody! He was anchored. He couldn't get . . .'

'He could y'know,' murmured Pilter.

'What?' Baxter's jaw slackened.

'Anything. That wheelchair was a con. Don't ask me why, just take my word. The post mortem. The pathologist. Gordon's legs were as good as yours, as good as mine, and he'd used 'em recently.' Pilter lifted his glass in mock-toast. 'Good luck, Baxter. You're likely to need it. You've a hell of a lot to worry about.'

Pilter drove more slowly on his return journey. He toyed with his thoughts; fingered them, much as a man whiling away the time might finger the scattered pieces of a jigsaw puzzle in the mild hope of finding a piece that fitted. The puzzle was still very incomplete; only the edges had been fitted together. The central part – the picture itself – had yet to take shape and colour.

Gordon, for example . . .

Forget the lunacy about the legs and the wheelchair. A chat with Gordon's medic might go a long way towards answering *that* question. Just concentrate on Gordon, the man . . . the personality. A mite nasty, perhaps. Domineering.

A man easily disliked. Perhaps easily hated. Certainly a man difficult to like, much less love. Some men *were* like that. Not deliberately . . . just naturally. Selfish. Self-satisfied. Arrogant. Incapable of seeing beyond the sphere of their own interests.

Gordon?

Could be . . . some men *were* like that.

THE DETECTIVE CHIEF SUPERINTENDENT (2)

Boredom. A bloody funny thing boredom. Damn-all to do with solitude, or even being alone; some of the happiest old boys in history hadn't had a soul within miles. But they hadn't been bored. The other thing in fact.

Whereas he . . .

Run off his arse sometimes. More work than he could handle . . . and work he enjoyed. Making the worms squirm. Putting the boot in and watching their eyes widen as they saw visions of iron bars and prison cells. Street-sweeping . . . in a manner of speaking. Clearing the streets of scum. Something to be proud of and something he could do well.

But bored out of his mind.

Why? For Christ's sake, why? Every day was just that little bit different, ergo no monotony. And who was kidding who? The monotony was there, all right. Monotony . . . and boredom. Like The Times *Crossword Puzzle. The first time took hours. Then when you'd cracked the real nut – when you'd figured out the workings of the minds of the men setting the crossword puzzle – after that it became easy. The question was no longer 'Whether?' The question was now 'How long?' Another name for boredom. A different problem – a different crossword puzzle – every day, but basically the same old questions and the same old answers.*

Maybe a wife might have changed things. Who knows?

All his buddies were married. Had kids. Had what they called 'home interests'.

Yeah – well . . . screw that for a tale!

Tommy Pilter was Tommy Pilter and it was a damn sight too late for a Mrs Tommy Pilter. Assuming, of course, he ever met the right female. Assuming, of course, some woman was mad enough to take him on after a life of bachelorhood. Assuming, of course . . . too many damn things. A lot too many things.

He was set in his ways, and happy.

But – hell! – he was bored.

Dr Austin had said, 'Of course I knew. There wasn't a thing wrong with his legs.'

'Then why the blazes . . .' Pilter had gasped non-understanding.

'The invalid chair?'

'It doesn't make sense.'

'To him.' Austin had moved the articles on his desk-top as he'd talked. His neatly manicured fingers had lined up pads of forms, a leather-covered, box-like container, pens, pencils, the small paraphernalia of his profession. Moved them, gently and geometrically, as he'd talked. 'To a rich man . . . and he was that. To a rich eccentric . . . you could call him that. A wheelchair. A nurse. Nothing illegal, surely?'

'Nothing illegal,' Pilter had agreed. 'But strange.'

'Some people like it that way. I have others. Four – perhaps five – all private patients. They have their foibles. It's a harmless form of self-indulgence.'

'But secretive.'

'With Gordon,' the doctor had agreed.

'There has to be a reason.'

'Master of his own destiny, perhaps?' The doctor had stopped his tidying long enough to glance questioningly at Pilter. He'd continued, 'That's an over-simplification, I know.

81

But basically it's a state of mind we come across periodically.'

'And his wife?'

'*I* didn't tell her. He asked me not to, so why should I?'

'The nurse?'

'Or the nurse.' The doctor had indulged in a slow, whimsical smile. 'She wasn't necessary, nor come to that was she a good nurse. Just one more prop to the false façade.'

'And you weren't even curious?'

'Curious.' The doctor had nodded. 'But not over-curious. I'm a busy man. And, moreover, I've known more irrational things . . . much more irrational. It was strange, but it was harmless.'

Strange, but harmless. A strange, but happy, harmless family; the Gordons and the Baxters. The hell they were! Definitely round the bend, at least some of 'em. Austin hadn't even been notified of the death; he'd read the news item in the local rag then later he'd been officially notified by some flatfoot or another. Not by Gordon's missus. Not by Baxter. Everything arse-about-face. *That* strange. *That* harmless.

Pilter braked the Rover and climbed out. He indulged himself in a few deep breaths. Good air. Crisp from the night's frost. To one side the shadow of the house stretched across the lawn and, where the low-slung sun hadn't yet touched, the grass was still white with hoar frost.

Pilter thumbed the bell-push, then flapped his arms as he waited. Celia Baxter answered his ring and led him into the lounge. Ruth Gordon and the nurse, Hulda Deschin, were both there; sipping tea and munching biscuits. The legendary British *sangfroid*; the head of the house had just snuffed it – at the moment he was stiff on a morgue slab having had cyanide removed from his guts – but so what? . . . 'elevenses' as usual.

Ruth Gordon said, 'Please sit down, Mr Pilter.'

Pilter lowered himself into an empty wing-chair.

'Tea?'

82

'No thanks.'

Pilter glanced at the faces of the three women. No red rims around any of the eyes. No catch in any of the voices. The poor bastard was dead, but these three weren't doing much mourning.

He said, 'Inspector Skeel tells me the inquest's this afternoon. At three.'

'He telephoned,' said Ruth Gordon.

'Opened and adjourned,' said Pilter.

'What does that mean exactly?'

'Evidence of identification. Evidence of cause of death. Then the coroner releases the body and you can go ahead with funeral arrangements.'

Ruth Gordon nodded her understanding.

'Cause of death,' murmured Celia Baxter.

'*Medical* cause of death. Cyanide poisoning. Not how it was administered . . . or who administered it.'

Ruth Gordon hesitated then said, 'We – er – we thought suicide.'

'Why?' Pilter smiled, innocently, as he asked the question.

Celia Baxter said, 'The wheelchair. He found it very frustrating.'

'Did he?'

'Well . . . wouldn't you?'

'I saw your husband yesterday,' said Pilter. 'Has he told you?'

'No.'

'Odd.'

'Not if you know my husband.' It was meant as a throwaway smile-line. But it wasn't.

'Tell me about your husband,' suggested Pilter.

'If you've already seen him . . .'

'I like as many opinions as possible.'

'You don't think it's sneaky?' There was scorn and antagonism in the question.

'A murder enquiry,' said Pilter gently.

'Is it?' asked Ruth Gordon.

'As near as dammit.' He turned to Celia Baxter and continued, 'Why not tell me about your husband?'

'You think Neil might have killed him?'

'I think somebody might.'

'Neil?'

'He's one of the front-runners.'

'You don't know my husband.'

'That's why I'm asking.'

'Assuming murder,' said Celia Baxter. 'Neil hasn't the guts.'

'Everybody has the guts,' said Pilter. 'There's a breaking-point. A different one for everybody. Reach the breaking-point . . . they have the guts. They *find* the guts from somewhere.'

'So you think Neil?' There was no shock in the question. Curiosity, perhaps, but no shock.

Pilter said, 'He was cooking the books.'

She inclined her head slightly.

'But,' added Pilter, 'I don't have to tell *you* that . . . do I?'

Ruth Gordon said, 'You don't have to tell anybody.' She turned to the nurse and said, 'Hulda. Will you leave us for a few minutes, please.'

The German girl bobbed her head, stood up and left the room.

As Pilter lighted a cigarette Ruth Gordon said, 'Mr Pilter, my sister and I have no secrets. *No* secrets.' She paused pointedly. She continued, 'We both know Neil. Probably better than he knows himself.'

' "Know" Neil,' murmured Pilter.

Celia Baxter said, 'Yes, that too.'

'You didn't mind?'

'Ruth's my sister. I still don't mind.'

'Does *he* know you know?' asked Pilter. 'Your husband, I mean.'

'Of course.'

'And Gordon?'

'Yes.' She nodded. 'He knew, too.'

'You are,' observed Pilter, 'a very broad-minded bunch.'

Ruth Gordon said, 'Love doesn't come into it, Mr Pilter. Don't make *that* mistake.'

'It never entered my head,' smiled Pilter.

Celia Baxter returned the smile and said, 'You really *don't* know my husband, do you?'

'I'm willing to learn.'

CELIA BAXTER (2)

So love doesn't come into it, big sister. Love doesn't come into it after all. That in front of a stranger. No hedging of bets. No pussy-footing around. You let my man take you to bed, but love doesn't come into it.

In hell's name, what does that make me?

That row. That almighty, cat-and-dog, eye-scratching, screaming row, when the animal told me. When he admitted – boasted – that his women included my own sister. My elder sister.

The names I called him. You wouldn't know. You . . . you've always figured yourself slightly superior. Older, therefore better. Better at what, kid? Better at lying? Better at keeping your cool? Better in bed, maybe? You wouldn't know, my beloved sister.

But, one thing, we never double-crossed each other. Faults? The two-legged stallion has faults like other men have hairs on their chest. But no back-door talk. No sweet nothings that add up to a big, fat lie.

He robbed your old man stupid. I knew it, you knew it,

85

but George never knew. George was played for a sucker all along the line.

Me? I'd have told tales. Bet on it, kid. The other way round – if Neil had been sitting there having the gold plate scraped from his hide – I'd have spilled the beans. Too damn true. Bed or no bed – bit on the side or no bit on the side – I wouldn't have stood by and watched my man taken for the complete mug.

The difference, sweet sister. The difference between you and me.

What was it I said? What was it?

'We don't get bitchy with each other about men, darling. Go ahead . . . keep it in the family. George might not mind as much.'

And you? You couldn't even recognise sarcasm when you heard it. So damn sure. So almighty bloody sure of yourself. Little sister – little Celia – wouldn't dare to get sarcy with you.

Yeah . . . well.

George didn't give a damn. Not a snap-of-the-fingers damn. I told him and I still remember his exact words.

'Celia, don't waste time tittle-tattling. Ruth's a grown woman with a mind of her own. What you should be doing is bringing Neil to heel, don't you think?'

And now this copper. This Pilter creep. 'Love doesn't come into it.' That's telling him, Ruth darling.

That's telling him . . . it's also telling me.

'You love your husband?' Pilter made it more of a question than a statement. He drew on his cigarette as he waited for Celia Baxter's answer.

She said, 'If it's any business of yours.'

'Let's say I'm morbidly curious.'

'Okay, let's say I love him.'

'Not just the sex thing.'

'Would you believe I'm not an animal, mister?'

'Despite the affair between him and your sister?'

'A she-camel . . . I'd still love the creep.'

'It's beyond me.' Pilter shook his head. 'It's *well* beyond me.'

'Sure.' She blinked. It was possible she was blinking back tears. In a voice low with suppressed emotion she said, 'You married? Happily married with lots of kids?'

'No. No kids. Not married.'

'It figures.' Her expression seemed to solidify; as if every tiny muscle of her face was suddenly under perfect control and held rigid. In some strange way it had an effect upon her voice, making it toneless and mechanical. She reached towards a lacquered box and table-lighter, slowly – deliberately – took a cigarette and, after the first deep inhalation of smoke, said, 'Masochism, mister. That's the medical name for it. They don't come worse. They don't come more selfish. But that's okay, it's okay because it *has* to be okay. Split? Leave him? So who sheds tears? Not boyo. He'll cry for nobody. Maybe himself, but sure as hell nobody else.

'You're a copper, mister. You've seen the miserable bitches. Their men beat them up. "Battered wives" they call them. And for every one leaving the bastard who's fisted hell out of them how many stay? Beatings and all . . . how many stay? *Why* do they stay? Answer that, mister policeman, and you're part-way to understanding why *I* don't leave.

'There's no reason. No reason on God's earth. No reason anybody not where I'm sitting will ever understand. He's a pig. He's an animal. He's a louse. Okay, he's all those things. He uses me as a doormat. He screws around . . . my own sister for Christ's sake. Okay, I still think he's the best man in the world. I'm in a minority of one. Maybe two, because he'd agree with me, but for different reasons. I'm still right, mister. I'm still *right*!'

She paused, drew deeply on the cigarette then, in little more than a whisper, ended, 'The nut doctors might be able to draw diagrams. I wouldn't know. I don't even care. A "child substitute", maybe. Don't think I haven't learned all the smart-arse answers. A "mother complex" because we don't have kids, but if so I've one hell of a delinquent for a son. But that's no matter, eh? Unlike this sister of mine, love comes into it. In a big way. I tell you . . . he tears my heart out with his bare hands *and I still worship the bastard*.'

Her face seemed to crumble, like a falling wall. She reached out a hand and squashed the cigarette into a nearby ash-tray, then the tears spilled and ran down the make-up on her cheeks. She dropped her head into her hands and her shoulders shook as the misery tore its way through her whole body.

Ruth Gordon made a movement to leave her chair.

'Leave her,' said Pilter gently.

'She's – she's . . .'

'She's dragged it out of her system. Better out than in.'

Ruth Gordon hesitated, then nodded, relaxed back in her chair and said, 'Perhaps.'

Pilter finished his cigarette then said, 'You offered tea.'

'What?' Ruth Gordon seemed to snap herself out of a dream.

'Tea. When I first arrived.'

'Oh, certainly. I'll call Hulda. She'll . . .'

'You,' smiled Pilter.

She looked puzzled but said, 'If you insist.'

'I think Miss Deschin should be kept out of things for the moment.'

Ruth Gordon nodded her understanding, stood up from her chair and left the room.

So as always the old, old problem. How to question a newly widowed wife without twisting the knife too savagely. Every time the same problem. Every time a different answer; an answer tailor-made for *that* woman.

Pilter knew coppers to whom the problem was no problem at all. Just go ahead and ask. Forget the hurt. Ignore the tears. Drag 'em through hell backwards, what's the odds as long as the questions are answered?

That of course was one way.

Not Pilter's way, at least not this time.

Murder. The problem was murder. And not 'Who?', but 'Whether?' Whether suicide or murder. Suicide was still a possibility, and more than a possibility. Any damn fool who claimed to be 'master of his own destiny' – to use Dr Austin's phrase – was by definition capable of taking his own life.

She'd carried the tray into the lounge, placed it handily on a small table, between the two chairs and asked, 'Shall I pour?'

Pilter had said, 'Please.'

'Milk?'

'Please.'

'Sugar?'

'Two lumps, please.'

There had been a strange domesticity about the episode; as if this had not been the first time they'd sat at a table to drink tea, munch buttered scones and converse with each other; as if this *tête-à-tête* had been but one more of a large number of similar pleasant meetings. She possessed that elusive quality – that inner tranquillity – capable of making the awkward and the near-embarrassing become natural and without difficulty.

At her entrance Celia Baxter had walked from the room without a word.

And Ruth Gordon had smiled, understandingly and murmured, 'Poor Celia. She has a difficult life. That's the first time I've known her break down in front of a stranger. I think she feels a little ashamed.'

Then she'd placed the tray on the table and asked, 'Shall I pour?'

Pilter felt his way gingerly; with what he considered caution mixed with cunning. He said, 'Your husband. We must talk about him, of course.'

'Of course.'

'Was he – er – religious in any way?' The question was asked in an almost off-handed tone.

'Religious?' She sounded astonished.

'Some people are,' he said gently.

'Yes, of course, but . . .' She stopped, then smiled and said, 'You mean the possibility of suicide?'

'It's a possibility,' agreed Pilter.

'No . . .' She spoke slowly. Thoughtfully. 'George wasn't religious. Not in the usual sense. Not a practising Christian . . . nothing like that.'

'But?' encouraged Pilter.

'He had some – er – very *personal* beliefs.'

Pilter said, 'He was once The Great Gordano, I believe?'

'Yes.' She nodded. 'Years ago.'

'I – er – I saw him once.'

'Really?'

'At The Prince of Wales Theatre. He took over the whole show.'

'Yes.' For a moment her eyes filmed as she gazed into the past. 'We were quite famous in those days.'

'We?'

'*He* was,' she corrected herself. 'I was one of his assistants. Herman Deschin – Hulda's father – and myself. We – er – helped with the tricks. Quite a company. More than thirty, including our own stage hands. But Herman and I were the chief assistants.'

'I see.' Pilter allowed a few moments of silence; time for her to disentangle herself from memories. Then he murmured, 'Religion?'

'No.' She shook her head. 'He wasn't a believer . . . in anything.'

'People usually are. Even if they don't flaunt their belief.'

'Not stage magicians,' she insisted.

'Really?'

'They perform their own miracles,' she smiled.

'I – er – I suppose they do.'

She said, 'Knowing George, he wouldn't have committed suicide.'

'Knowing *people*.' Pilter paused, then added, 'Anybody.'

'Not George,' she insisted.

Pilter compressed his lips, raised his eyebrows then, in a wry tone, said:

'That leaves . . . murder.'

She nodded.

'Who?' asked Pilter quietly. Then he continued, 'Also why the change of heart?'

'I'm sorry?'

'When I first arrived. Less than an hour ago. You expressed an opinion . . . suicide.'

'No.' She shook her head. 'As I recall I said "*We* thought suicide". Celia, Hulda, myself. They're so sure. I was doubtful . . . the remark was made for their benefit.'

'I find that odd, Mrs Gordon.'

'From what you've said. From the way you've said it. "Murder . . . as near as dammit". That was *your* expression. It convinced me.'

'Just like that?'

'You are the expert.'

'Okay.' Pilter tasted some tea. 'Let's say – as an expert – I plump for suicide. Your husband was a conjurer. An illusionist. He could palm things, right?'

She nodded.

Pilter continued. 'He palmed the used condom packet, dropped the cyanide into the drink, slipped the empty packet into Baxter's breast pocket. For a man with his dexterity simple, surely?'

'If he was capable of suicide.'

'On the assumption that he *was* capable.'

'In that case.' She nodded. 'Moderately simple.'

'So?'

'He *was* in a wheelchair.'

'True. But, as I understand things, there was a fair amount of movement. People passing him. Baxter passing him.'

'Yes.' She seemed to be undecided. She looked worried, then said, 'It's confusing, Mr Pilter. Celia has a point. He was a chair-borne invalid. Obviously, it was frustrating. Equally obviously it was . . .'

'No.' The interruption was harsh. Cold. It had a strange echoing quality; like something dropped in an empty room.

Ruth Gordon's eyes opened slightly.

Pilter stared into the widened eyes and said, 'Do I have to tell you, Mrs Gordon. Do I have to tell *you*?'

'What?'

'About the chair?'

'What about the chair? What was wrong with the chair?'

'Not a thing. The chair was in perfect working order . . . so was the *man* in the chair.'

FLASHBACK

The same family – the Mayer family – had run the Hôtel
Beau Rivage since 1865. They were rightly proud; it was a
fine hotel alongside Lake Geneva; it specialised in French
cuisine and exquisite wines. Of necessity only the very rich
could afford to hold a wedding reception at the Hôtel Beau
Rivage but (of equal necessity) what wedding receptions *were*
held there carried with them the dream-like quality of something from An Arabian Night's Entertainment.

The Great Gordano and his new wife were happy beyond
their wildest imaginings. Their guests – the whole company,
friends and relations – were all a little intoxicated by the
sheer, money-no-object magnificence of the food and the
drink and the service.

Eight-year-old little Hulda Deschin sat, wide-eyed and
stunned at this real-life fairyland. Hardly able to believe that
such truly beautiful dresses – such genuine happiness – could
be part of a world which also included the drabness – the
smouldering bitterness – of her native Berlin.

Herman Deschin smiled down at her. He rested a hand
on her shoulder and said, 'My Hulda. It really *is*, you know.
Peace, my darling. Peace and security, here in our own little
world.'

Meanwhile in another corner of the great room, Celia Col-
ster was saying similar things to her newly married sister.

'I'm happy for you, Ruth. Really happy. You'll have a

good life . . . I know you will. All this. It's George's promise that you're *really* under his protection now. Not just one of the troupe any more. His wife. His very special responsibility. I know men, Ruth, I know men like George. They set their own standards. They're – they're like gold . . . as precious as gold. That's why I'm happy for you. So happy for you.'

And, indeed, the happiness was there. It was no empty promise on the part of The Great Gordano. Throughout the world his name was in lights. His illusions were the wonder of lesser stage magicians. He could fill a theatre for weeks on end, he could perform his magic on the aprons of famous night-clubs or even within the closed confines of a circus ring. There seemed to be nothing he could not make vanish or re-appear from thin air.

And always the nucleus of the same company. His 'family' as he called them. Herman Deschin and his wife, Ruth, were his two main assistants; without them the more spectacular of his illusions would have been impossible. They knew his secrets and kept his secrets, and he in turn showed lavish gratitude. He arranged and paid for the schooling of Hulda Deschin and, when she expressed a desire to enter the nursing profession, he arranged that, too.

Meanwhile, they toured. Every country – every capital – in Europe. Every major city in America. Australia, New Zealand, Canada, South Africa. And always to capacity houses.

The Great Gordano. To the members of 'The Gordano Company' that word 'Great' had a very special meaning.

In 1958 Herman Deschin died; he died in Las Vegas, suddenly and as the indirect result of a British bullet which had penetrated his chest in the North African desert. The whole company mourned his passing, but Gordano did more than merely mourn. He arranged for the body to be transported back to Deschin's beloved Berlin; arranged and paid for a decent interment; took over the immediate guardianship

94

of the orphaned Hulda . . . and as far as was possible eased the hurt.

Thus the magnanimity of The Great Gordano.

But he demanded something in return. He demanded absolute and immediate obedience. He demanded complete loyalty. Within the troupe he claimed near-despotic authority, and it was granted him and never grudgingly.

Indeed, if he were a despot, he was a very enlightened despot. He was a friend of presidents and a confidant of men in high places. He had power and, although he never abused that power, neither did he hesitate to use it on behalf of his 'family'.

All this until April, 1966.

LONGER LOOK (PART TWO)

But men must know, that in this
theatre of man's life it is reserved
only for God and angels to be
lookers-on.

Advancement of Learning
Francis Bacon

Pilter swallowed a couple of indigestion tablets and wondered when the hell ulcers would be acknowledged as an 'industrial disease' as far as the Police Service was concerned. All this worry. All this faffing around. All this bloody red tape.

And along there in his own office the paper-work would by this time be sky-high. Form This, Form That, Form The Other . . . more blasted forms than Soft Mick. And on every one of 'em – there in the bottom right-hand corner – the box-space waiting for *his* signature. The buck-stops-here spot.

One bloody day . . .

He burped gently as he tapped on the chief constable's office door.

A voice from within called, 'Come.'

Pilter opened the door, closed it behind him, then accepted the invitation as the chief constable waved a hand towards a chair.

'Well?' asked the chief.

'Opened and adjourned, as expected.'

'Good.' The chief sounded satisfied.

'Depends where you're standing,' growled Pilter.

'I'm sorry. I'm not with you.'

'It's murder . . . I reckon.'

'You still have doubts?'

'Suicide – some fancy form of suicide – can't be ruled out.'

'Er – "fancy"?'

'Most insurance companies don't pay out on suicide. They cough up on murder, but not suicide. Gordon might have wanted it to *look* like murder.'

99

'Unnecessary tom-foolery,' observed the chief.

'Gordon,' murmured Pilter. 'The Great Gordano . . . remember him?'

'The magician chap? Haven't heard of him for years.'

'Gordon.'

'Good Lord!'

'That's what makes it a possibility,' explained Pilter.

'Suicide?'

'It's possible. Commits suicide in front of witnesses. Makes it look like murder.'

'Ah!'

Very helpful (thought Pilter). He sits there like a pregnant duck and says 'Ah!'. Very bloody constructive. There's now a coroner in the background, and that coroner wants a firm decision – one way or the other – and all this blimp-faced berk can say is 'Ah!'.

Pilter said, 'The pathologist mentioned the legs.'

'Gordon's legs?'

'That the wheelchair wasn't necessary.'

'Oh, I see. Any comment?'

'Not officially. Unofficially a lot of speculation.'

'By whom?'

'The reporters. Just about everybody.'

'The coroner?'

'The coroner wants to know,' said Pilter heavily.

'About the legs?'

'About the death. Suicide or murder. He's eager to get the record straight.'

'Naturally.'

Pilter said, 'Naturally.'

'What?'

'The coroner. All he does is sit on his elegant arse telling everybody to get their records straight. So naturally, it comes easy.'

'I, too, would like to see the record straight, Mr Pilter.'

'Me, also. What do you suggest, chief constable? Tossing a coin?'

'Six suspects.' The chief made it sound like falling off a log.

'Six,' agreed Pilter.

'You should have some idea.'

'It's a pity,' said Pilter nastily. 'It's a great pity we can't shove all six in a dock and let a jury decide. Unfortunately, that's not allowed. But – for your personal information – your friend, Baxter, leads the field at the moment . . . just.' He paused, then added, 'If it isn't suicide, of course.'

The chief constable frowned then said, 'Ah!' again.

And of course Skeel had had to come up with another lead to follow. Trust Skeel. Trust the praiseworthy Skeel to trot along with one more monkey-wrench with which to gum up the machinery.

'Dearden. Raymond Dearden, the photographer.'

'What about him?'

'The poison registers. There's a record of him buying potassium cyanide ten days ago.'

'Dearden?'

'Yes.'

'Under his own name?'

'Yes.'

'Good.' Pilter had tried to look pleased. Then he'd said, 'Okay, inspector, now sniff out the filthy lucre angle.'

'Sir?'

'Check what insurance Gordon carried.'

'Which company?'

'God knows.' Pilter's tone had edged slightly towards the sarcastic. 'A man like you . . . tracing the company should be like sucking gum drops.'

Which was why Pilter was following the slim, pale-faced fairy up narrow, winding stairs, to a second-storey flat-cum-studio . . . and was also why Pilter was feeling more than a little aggrieved at the thought of yet one more evening screwed up to hell.

Like its occupant, the flat was distinctly gay. Eye-searing, almost. As if to make up for his own pallor Dearden had surrounded himself with garish colour. Scatter cushions. A couch-cum-bed with a vivid orange coverlet. Cane-chairs carefully drenched in blue, green and red. Everything had a no-half-measures colour; harsh, shiny and brittle. The end result was something not too far removed from a freshly-painted fairground roundabout.

Without being asked Pilter sat on the edge of the bed. Dearden lowered himself slowly into one of the cane-chairs.

'Well?' he asked.

'Potassium cyanide,' said Pilter.

'What about it?'

'You bought some recently.'

'What about it?' repeated Dearden.

Pilter suppressed a sigh and said, 'George Gordon died. Potassium cyanide poisoning. You were there at the time . . . remember?'

'Oh, my God!' Dearden almost threw up his arms.

'Okay. Tell me.'

'I'm a professional photographer for God's sake.'

'And?'

'I use the stuff all the time.'

'Is that a fact?'

'Didn't you *know*?' There was near-disbelief in the question.

'I might have guessed,' growled Pilter.

'What?'

'Knowing Skeel.'

'I'm sorry, I don't . . .'

'Nevertheless,' interrupted Pilter, 'you do handle the stuff.'

'All the time.'

102

'And you *were* at the Gordons' place when he snuffed it.'

'I thought . . .' Dearden closed his mouth suddenly.

'You thought what?'

'No, it doesn't matter.'

'It matters, Dearden. Anything remotely concerned with Gordon or that night matters.'

'I . . .' Dearden fluttered his fingers a little. 'I thought Baxter. Obviously.'

'Why Baxter?'

'He's – he's the type . . . isn't he?'

'*Is* there a type?' asked Pilter innocently.

Dearden said, 'It *could* have been suicide . . . have you thought?'

'Yeah. I've thought.'

'He wasn't a moderate man.'

'Er – moderate?'

'Gordon. Very bashy. You wouldn't believe.'

Pilter said, 'I'm still not with you.'

'Well now . . .' Dearden moved his hands as an aid to expression. 'I'm a photographer, see? An artist, though I say it myself. I have this theory. It's more than a theory, really. I *know*. Colour. Very yucky. It's never quite *right*. Black, white . . . with infinite degrees of grey. The effect's fantastic. If it's done right. It can . . .'

'What in blazes,' interrupted Pilter, 'has this to do with Gordon's death.'

'He wouldn't wear it,' said Dearden sadly.

'The colour thing?'

'An absolute cretin. A perfect cow. He wouldn't even *look*.'

'Hardly a reason for committing suicide, though.'

'Oh . . . I don't *know*.'

'For Christ's sake! Nobody commits suicide because they don't like the look of a photograph.'

'*I've* seriously contemplated it sometimes.'

Pilter stared, cleared his throat, then growled, 'Let's get back to Mother Earth, shall we. One at a time. Who had access to this place? Who visited? Baxter?'

'Sometimes. When he wanted to be particularly slimy.'

'Slimy?'

'Art studies. He called them art studies . . . as if *he* knows anything about art.'

'Dirty pictures?'

'You wouldn't believe.'

'I'd believe,' grunted Pilter. 'And?'

'What?'

'Did you ever oblige?'

'My God, no. I've my reputation to think about.'

'But he visited?'

Dearden nodded.

'So he could have nicked some potassium cyanide?'

'If . . .' Dearden hesitated, looked a little scared, then said, 'He *could* have. I'm not saying he *did*, but he could have.'

'Okay, Baxter. What about Mrs Baxter?'

Dearden said, 'I'm doing some Christmas cards for her.'

'Christmas cards?'

'Something personal. Still life. She wants fifty. I've made half-a-dozen postcard-size blow-ups. Various ideas. She hasn't decided.'

'So *she's* been up here?'

'Oh, yes.' Dearden smiled. 'A nice lady.'

'I wouldn't know.'

'With a thing like Baxter as a husband . . . I don't know how she copes.'

'She seems to get along.'

'Yes, that's what I mean.'

'But *she* could have helped herself to the stuff?'

'I don't see why she . . .'

'*Could* she?' insisted Pilter.

104

With obvious reluctance, Dearden muttered, 'Yes, she *could*. If it had been her husband who'd . . .'

'It wasn't her husband. It was Gordon. What about Mrs Gordon?'

'The potassium cyanide?'

'That's what we're on about.'

'She – er – she visits sometimes. About once a fortnight.'

'Christmas cards?'

'No.' Dearden's expression became sulky. Like that of an over-indulged child. He said, 'Gordon could be very nasty sometimes. Very hurtful. She – er – she came to apologise.'

'For her husband?'

'Yes. She's a very understanding person.'

'Understanding?'

'She knows what it's like to be hurt.'

'Does she?' The question contained some surprise.

'With Gordon, I mean,' amplified Dearden. 'He could be really horrid. Dictatorial. His own way . . . or nothing.'

'With his wife, too?'

'I suppose so. Those sort of men don't know the meaning of the word "gentleness". And,' he went on hurriedly, 'don't start on about that silly invalid chair. He's not the only one in the world. Other people have crosses to bear. It doesn't make them *all* inhuman.'

RAYMOND DEARDEN (2)

Good riddance, that's what he said. Good riddance. The world could do with a few less George Gordon types. Not that he wished anybody dead. Not that. But – y'know – it would be a better world.

As it was people like him (Raymond Dearden) – people like him – always at the receiving end of dirty remarks. Snide

105

insults. As if he hadn't any feelings, for God's sake. As if he didn't matter. As if he couldn't be hurt.

Well, he did hurt. He hurt very easily. He was an artist – which was something Gordon couldn't appreciate – so he hurt very easily.

So good riddance. That was one less person able to hurt him.

And for the life of him, he couldn't see Gordon's wife being too heartbroken. Oh, yes, she'd have to put on some sort of show. Of course she would. Tears. Black. All the rest of it. But inside – inside, y'know – she had to be glad. Well, if not glad, relieved. She had to be relieved. A woman with feelings. A woman who understood. She had to be relieved at the release from a cretin like George Gordon.

This potassium cyanide thing, though . . .

That was very awkward, wasn't it? I mean he (Raymond Dearden) used the stuff by the pound. By the ton! It was poison – of course it was poison, any fool knew that. But it was part of his profession and he kept quite a bit on hand. Just in case he needed some in a hurry. And that old fool Gordon had to go get himself poisoned with the stuff.

It was awkward, wasn't it?

It put him (Raymond Dearden) in a very peculiar position, didn't it?'

'Did *you* poison him?' asked Pilter suddenly.

'What?' Dearden's eyes widened. His jaw dropped.

'You?' said Pilter pleasantly.

'You have to be joking.'

'No.' Pilter shook his head. 'You didn't like the guy. You have cyanide handy. It's the obvious question. Did *you* poison him?'

'I did *not*!'

'Some silly bugger did,' observed Pilter mildly. He seemed to switch subjects and asked, 'Do you use condoms?'

106

'What?' Dearden's eyes widened even more.

'Condoms. French letters. You and Hector. I'm a bit hazy on these things. Do you?'

'That's a – a – a *disgusting* question to ask.'

'Ain't it, though?' Pilter's grin carried overtones of lasciviousness. 'Nevertheless answer it.'

'I'm – hardly likely to become pregnant, am I?'

'That's a fact,' agreed Pilter.

'So, does that answer your question?'

'I reckon.'

'In that case, why ask it?'

'Let's say I've a dirty mind,' said Pilter.

'If you've come here to . . .'

'Potassium cyanide.'

'What?'

'That's why I'm here. What killed Gordon. The "agent" as it's known in flash circles. You don't buy it at the corner tobacconist's along with a packet of fags. Bobbying – first principle in a poisoning job – find where the "agent" might have come from. Second principle, find who had access to the "agent". Obvious when you think about it. That's why dumb-bells like me can make chief superintendent. Okay, I've traced the possible – *probable* – source of the "agent". Suspects? Yourself. Baxter. Mrs Baxter. Mrs Gordon. Dobson . . . does he visit?'

'Sometimes. Occasionally.' Dearden's spat of outrage had turned into sullen antagonism.

'Sometimes. Occasionally,' repeated Pilter. 'How occasional is "sometimes"?'

'He comes to see John.'

'Hector?'

'That's his only reason for visiting here.'

'And the last time?'

'About ten days ago.'

'Tell me about Dobson,' invited Pilter.

107

'He's a drummer.'

'Yeah, he's also on grass. Right?'

'I wouldn't know.'

'Pot,' explained Pilter.

'I know what "grass" means.'

'Dobson smokes the stuff.'

'Does he?'

'D'you have secrets then?' asked Pilter.

'Who?'

'You and Hector.'

'I don't see how Hec . . .'

'Hector knows Dobson smokes the muck. He must know. You and Hector. That's what I mean.'

'All right. I know Dobson's on pot. Who isn't these days?'

'You?'

'I wouldn't touch the filthy stuff.' The look of disgust amplified the truth of the answer.

'Right, *now* tell me about Dobson.'

'He's . . .' Dearden tilted his head slightly, closed his eyes, then said, 'He's a yuck. An absolute yuck.' He opened his eyes, kept his nose slightly elevated and raised his eyebrows. 'You've seen him. What do *you* think?'

'A yuck,' agreed Pilter and kept a straight face.

'Of course. He calls himself a drummer. My God . . . a *drummer*. He's only in The Ectoplasm because John's too soft-hearted to give him the big E. *And* he knows it.'

'Does he?'

'Gordon didn't like him.'

'Really?'

'Gordon wanted to send him packing months ago. *Years* ago.'

'Gordon?'

'Gordon wanted to.' Dearden nodded. 'But John runs The Ectoplasm, not Gordon. And John's too soft-hearted.'

'What would happen,' asked Pilter gently, 'if Dobson lost his place in this group thing? This Ectoplasm?'

'He doesn't deserve a place.'

'Okay, what if he lost it?'

'He'd be nowhere.'

'Out of work?'

'He wouldn't be a drummer, that's for sure. Nobody else would want him.'

'So . . .' pondered Pilter. 'We have a pot-head. A yuck. And this yuck – this pot-head – knows he's out in the cold if Gordon can influence your pal Hector. This yuck also has access to potassium cyanide . . . and Gordon dies from a dose of potassium cyanide.' Pilter looked questioningly at Dearden. He murmured, 'Comments. please.'

'My God!' breathed Dearden.

'Pot,' Pilter reminded him. 'No work, no pot.'

'He . . .' Dearden swallowed, then said, 'He *could*.'

'The right type?'

'I – I think so.'

'You were there,' said Pilter. 'Opportunity?'

'He *could*,' repeated Dearden. 'There was a lot of – y'know – moving around.'

'So I've heard.'

'It's – y'know – possible.'

'Possible,' sighed Pilter. 'And what's "possible"? One step short of "probable" and "probable" isn't far from "too damn right"?'

'I didn't say that,' objected Dearden.

'No. I did. I'm paid to say those sort of things . . . to *think* those sort of things.'

Or am I?

Pilter sprawled in the battered but comfortable armchair in front of his own electric fire, sipped hot toddy and gave serious thought to his own place in the scheme of things.

Am I? He thought. *Am I paid to play God? To take circumstantial bricks and, without the mortar of hard evidence, build a wall of guilt.*

Not forgetting, of course, all that crap about Presumption of Innocence.

Crap. Pure crap. Very nice in textbooks, but a non-starter when the *real* lawyers – the fighting lawyers – face each other in a Crown Court. Those twelve jurors. They look at the guy in the dock and before they even take the bloody oath they've mentally found the poor sod guilty. He wouldn't be standing there otherwise. He did it, she did it, otherwise he/she wouldn't be on trial. Because our police are wonderful. They don't make mistakes. They're always sure – *bloody* sure – before they shove some quaking bastard up there to be tried by his so-called 'peers'.

My aching back!

Okay, they're right, sometimes. But sometimes they're wrong. Sometimes – wheels within wheels – some poor shit-house is stood there because somebody *has* to be stood there. Because of the crime. Because of public opinion. Because of pressures: from the press, from parliament, from *anywhere*. What the hell? He's a yob, he's as bent as Spaghetti Junction, he's a list as long as your arm, he's better off the streets . . . and he *might* have done it. Let's just say he *did*. Let's stack the deck a little. Let's give him a little push.

Because some crimes *can't* be marked 'Undetected' . . . ever.

The wrong guy? So what? He's been asking for it all his life, okay, now he knows.

And the *right* guy gets the message, retires to a quiet corner and doesn't chance his arm again.

All his life Pilter had been haunted by a ghost. Maybe more than one ghost. How many? The sixty-four-thousand-dollar question. How many ghosts?

All those men he'd slammed behind granite. Young coppers; young coppers like Pilter had been; young detectives straight from the tag-end of World War II. Who the hell has a conscience worth a damn immediately after a war? The blood runs hot, the chase is the only thing you have in mind . . . who the hell *really* worries about which quarry you run to earth?

The law of averages, friend. That old law of averages . . . some of 'em *had* to have been innocent.

Okay, the book says 'Don't get involved'. The book says 'Don't think', 'Don't let it become too big a part of your life'. Some advice! The days stretch out to months, the months stretch out to years and the years stretch out forever . . . and don't let *that* become part of your life.

All your life, mister book-writer. All your life.

And when the rank is detective chief superintendent – when the position is Head of C.I.D. – and when you're honest enough to face facts (albeit in the secrecy of your own home and in the comfort of your own armchair) – the robins all come home to roost. Every doubt. Every 'Presumption of Innocence' that strictly speaking wasn't. Every 'maybe' and every 'perhaps'.

One hell of a time for self-recrimination, come to that. One hell of a time for qualms. One hell of a year; more than fifty-five years of age and a few years past voluntary retirement. One hell of an hour; three o'clock one November morning.

Yeah, well.

There has to *be* a time. There has to *be* one specific moment.

Why not now? Right *now*?

Pilter finished the hot toddy at a final gulp. And still his mind spun and spluttered. It happened sometimes – not too often, but sometimes – and never before as badly as this.

The Gordon case had brought things to a head. The Gordon case. Unusual for so many reasons. A one-man-band

111

affair; two possible verdicts, six possible suspects; no need for any other copper to even lick his pencil. Just him . . . Pilter. With Skeel doing what little footwork it required. Like The Great Gordano, in fact. The main magician . . . aided by one assistant. A murder enquiry, on a par with a conjuring trick. That's what made it so unusual. So unique. So bloody *difficult*.

Because if he was wrong . . .

'This,' said the chief constable with some pique, 'is a bit sudden.'

Pilter said, 'I'm getting old. I'd like to spend however many nights I have left in bed.'

'One month,' grumbled the C.C.

'That's what the regulations say.'

'A month's no time at all.'

'Half-a-dozen men,' said Pilter. 'At least half-a-dozen. All ready and eager to step into my shoes.'

'Possibly.'

'I'll send you a list.'

'Don't bother.' The chief constable held the typed resignation in his left hand, flicked it with the forefinger of his right hand and said, 'I still think this is very underhand. You could have given me some warning.'

'You're giving me more credit than I deserve,' said Pilter.

'Eh?'

'The force won't fall apart just because I've resigned.'

'Of course it won't.' The C.C. scowled then, almost grudgingly, added, 'Nevertheless we'll miss you.'

'Pick a young 'un,' advised Pilter.

'What?'

'A death-or-glory type. Let one of *them* have a go.'

'Mmm.' The chief frowned at the typewritten sheet, then said, 'There's still the Gordon affair.'

'Suicide,' lied Pilter.

'Really.' The chief looked up. Surprised. 'You've established that have you?'

'Uhu.' Pilter nodded. 'Six of 'em . . . each one with five eye-witnesses ready to clear any suggestion of hokey-pokey. It *has* to be suicide.'

'I – er – I suppose.' The chief wasn't quite convinced.

'Gordon was a nutter,' said Pilter. 'Round the twist. Inside he was still The Great Gordano. Even when he did himself in he had to do it the fancy way. One more mystery. One more sleight-of-hand.'

'I see.' The chief sounded happier. 'And the reason?'

'His missus was having it off with Baxter. There wasn't a thing Gordon could do about it. So two birds with one stone – he tried to make trouble for Baxter. The condom packet in Baxter's pocket.'

'Nasty,' observed the C.C.

'Not nice,' agreed Pilter.

'Good job you spotted it.'

'Aye.'

'Well.' The chief sounded philosophical. 'It rounds things off, I suppose. Nothing outstanding . . . this resignation, I mean. Whoever takes over starts with a clean slate.'

'More or less.'

'Leave?' asked the chief.

Pilter said, 'I've a few weeks owing. I'll empty all the baskets then take off.'

'Good.' The chief nodded. 'Just let me know when.'

THE DETECTIVE CHIEF SUPERINTENDENT (3)

So that made him a fool, eh? A conscience-ridden, sentimental old fool. Or on the other hand a gutless bastard. A man unwilling to do his job, just because sometime in the past –

113

just maybe – he'd done that same job a little too enthusias-
tically.

So who the hell cared?

Knead the old mind around a little and it didn't take too
much to see it as a levelling of the balance. At some time in
the past the wrong guy convicted – that in one pan of the
scales – and now the right guy getting away with it – that in the
other pan of the scales. A sort of rough-and-ready justice,
more or less.

Not that it mattered too much.

This one wasn't a hardened criminal. This one was no
rip-roaring tearaway; somebody the police would have to
fight every day of his remaining life. Just the one killing . . .
that's all.

And come to that who the hell could prove it? Prove it in
court? Where was the evidence? The real evidence? The hard,
hold-it-and-handle-it evidence?

An acquittal, for sure. The usual public washing of dirty
linen . . . then an acquittal. A very expensive show, paid for
by the police.

And that was another thing . . .

Y'know . . . The Great Gordano. That evening at The
Prince of Wales Theatre. So many years ago. A small life-
time ago. But one of those shows you never forget.

A small and belated 'thank you' to a man now dead; to
the man responsible for that never-to-be-forgotten show. Not
to drag his name through the muck of a court hearing. To
let him stay 'George Gordon'. To keep 'The Great Gordano'
up there in blazing lights . . . as always, the best.

Reasons.

A whole cart-load of reasons. All of them wrong. But add
them together and they became 'right' . . . maybe.

When he arrived back at his office Skeel was waiting for him.

Skeel said, 'He was worth about a quarter-of-a-million,

114

with about half as much again in insurance coverage. A two-way policy. Himself and his wife.'

'You've been busy,' said Pilter.

'Knowing who to ask.' Skeel almost preened himself. 'His accountant . . . off the record, of course. But with it being a murder enquiry.'

'It isn't,' said Pilter flatly.

'What?' Skeel's heels nearly left the carpet.

'Suicide.'

'Who on earth says . . .'

'The chief. D'you want to argue with him?'

'Well – er – no. But how does he . . .'

'Is it so important?'

'What?'

'Proving the top office wrong?'

'No, good Lord, no!' Pilter almost smiled at the speed with which Skeel back-tracked. 'It's – it's no skin off my nose. If the chief constable says "Suicide" . . . that's it.'

Pilter said, 'Fix it with the coroner. Gordon spiked his own drink, then slipped the condom packet into Baxter's pocket. Tried to make it look like murder . . . in case the insurance people jibbed at paying out on suicide.'

'Yes, of course.' Skeel nodded furiously. 'That's *obviously* what happened, obviously.'

'All this work for sod-all,' taunted Pilter.

'What?'

'Obvious, as you say. If it was so bloody obvious, why didn't you spot it before pulling the plunger?'

'I – I – I . . .'

Pilter said, 'Wrap it up in pink ribbon, Skeel. Close the file.'

'Oh, yes. Surely.'

'And – y'know – keep away from the chief for a few days. He tends to spit whenever he mentions your name.'

'Oh!'

'It'll wear off.' Pilter smiled. 'Just do the right thing from now on. He'll soon learn to love you again.'

'Yes. I'll – I'll see to it. Right away.'

Skeel scurried from his office and Pilter grinned at the closed door. Skeel ran on tram-lines. Skeel could be relied on to do 'the right thing' . . . look after Skeel.

The 'In' tray was full. What else? Two – three – days without the signatory-in-chief scrawling his name at the foot of each piece of bumpf. The wonder was that the production line hadn't been brought to a halt by a build-up of blasted forms.

He grunted, pulled the basket nearer to the desk-blotter, flopped down into the swivel-chair, plucked the fancy ballpoint from its holder and, without so much as glancing at the contents, signed each form in turn before tossing it into the 'Out' tray.

Not the way to do things, of course. Not at all the way to do things. But the way he'd *yearned* to do it ever since he'd first walked into the infernal office. Bobbying with a ballpoint . . . about as much as it was worth.

Because . . .

Damn it, the Gordon affair still had some loose ends. Some unanswered questions. Some bits and pieces of puzzle not yet in place.

Pilter muttered, 'For Christ's sake!', pushed himself out of the chair and prowled to the glass-fronted bookcase. He opened the doors and, from the bottom shelf, lifted out a black-bound volume. The gilt lettering on the spine read, *Medical Jurisprudence and Toxicology, Glaister, Eighth Edition.*

It was no modern textbook. That particular edition was damn near forty years old. Nevertheless . . .

Pilter checked through the index, then turned to Chapter Twelve. Without leaving the bookcase, he read the first page

116

of that chapter – then re-read it . . . then wondered what the hell the medical terms meant anyway.

He returned the book to its place, closed the bookcase doors and left the office.

What the hell else, they worked. Every muscle seemed to quiver and jerk; every pore seemed to spout its own tiny fountain of sweat. The combined onslaught of noise from the four guitars made Pilter's eardrums almost ache and the swirling, dancing galaxy of coloured spotlights added extra weight to the blatantly primitive drive of each succeeding 'number'.

The Ectoplasm was in top gear and swinging.

It hadn't been too difficult to find where the group was performing that night; a telephone call to Baxter then, as a small extra, Baxter's offer to drive him there and arrange for complimentary tickets.

One of the many night-clubs-cum-entertainment-emporiums which during the past few years had brought a new form of vaudeville to the northern provinces. You paid an entrance fee, you sat at a neat little table, you ate a good meal, you drank good booze . . . and you were entertained. Las Vegas style. Acts which toured the world; sometimes acts which only these gilt-edged clubs could afford to put on. The best acts of their kind . . . with back-up acts which were themselves way ahead of the also-rans.

'Okay?' Baxter had to ask the question in a near-shout.

'Noisy,' observed Pilter.

'Not your bag?' Baxter grinned.

'As long as the aspirins don't run out.' Pilter returned the grin.

They'd eaten well and now they were sipping brandy and black coffee and smoking cigarettes. Around them the chatter of small-talk and the clink of cutlery and crockery could be heard – just! – as a background of almost-normality to the din being thrown out from the apron stage.

Baxter leaned forward and said, 'Hector thinks this is too old-fashioned. Too run-of-the-mill.'

'What has he in mind? A re-run of Arnhem?'

Baxter thought the remark funny. The grin was replaced by an open-mouthed, head-thrown-back laugh.

Baxter (thought Pilter) had better laugh while the laughing was good because, unless he (Pilter) was much mistaken, the time for laughter was strictly limited. When the boom dropped, the funnies ended.

Meanwhile, the ten-cylinder racket which masqueraded as 'modern popular music' continued to make the walls vibrate and Pilter hoped to hell the top of his skull was anchored firmly into place, pending a session with Hector in the dressing-rooms.

John Hector's body gleamed sweat as he tipped the contents of a beer can down his gullet. He was naked except for a pair of light blue jockey shorts. His body was a thing of whipcord and supple muscles; an athlete's body and (presumed Pilter) kept in peak condition via the expenditure of energy needed for The Ectoplasm act. His beard and hair were still frizzed from the towelling they'd received, prior to him stripping away his clothes and throwing them into an untidy heap on a dressing-room chair.

'Yeah?' Hector dried his mouth with the back of a hand. 'Some questions you want to ask . . . right?'

'Right.' Pilter took a packet of cigarettes from his pocket, offered them to Hector, then flicked a lighter and touched the flame to both cigarettes. He said, 'A few questions. About Gordon. Any objections?'

'Should I have?' Hector held the cigarette in his mouth as he towelled the sweat from his body, arms and legs. He said, 'You see the act?'

118

'Uhu?' Pilter nodded.

'What d'you think?'

'Baxter put it in a nutshell. Not my bag.'

'Nor mine.'

'Really?' Pilter raised surprised eyebrows.

'All that noisy shit.' Hector towelled under his armpits. 'I'm *there*, in the middle of it – it damn near drives me nuts.'

'In that case, why?'

'Why anything? Bread. What else?' Hector tossed the towel onto the discarded clothes, removed the cigarette from his mouth and hitched a buttock onto the edge of the wall-shelf dressing-table. He said, 'Would you believe I had training. Real training. Classical guitar . . . the whole musical works.'

'And this?'

'I was good.' Hector inhaled tobacco smoke. 'Good, but not great. Good enough to know I'd never *be* great. This garbage pays. Unfortunately.' He pulled an exaggerated wry face. 'The goons who like it don't know the difference. I put good chord-work in out there. If I was plucking a one-stringed fiddle they'd still clap, if it was loud enough.'

'We all have our problems,' murmured Pilter.

'Ain't that a fact?'

'And – correct me if I'm wrong – one of *your* problems was George Gordon.'

'Er . . .' Hector hesitated, then smiled and said, 'Yeah. One of the lesser problems.'

'Tell me,' invited Pilter.

'He had a contract,' said Hector slowly. 'Not cast-iron . . . tempered steel. He was a good agent. One of the best. And if you needed a good agent – and who doesn't? – Gordon was your man. But that contract was part of the deal. It told you when. It told you where. It told you how. It damn near included your heartbeat.'

'You found it – er – restrictive?'

119

'Yeah. Y'see . . .' Hector drew deeply on the cigarette. 'I have this thing. This great idea. The crappy tunes the kids go for these days . . . nothing! No melody. No class. Nothing they can latch onto, until it's been thrown at them a few thousand times by every D.J. on the take. But the tunes are there, friend. Great tunes. Fabulous tunes. Melody-lines nobody *ever* forgets. Beethoven, Grieg, Mozart, Brahms. More melodies than one man could ever handle in a lifetime. Rearrange them . . . *good* arrangements. And the right beat, the right electronic interplay . . . and that's *it*.'

Pilter said, 'It's been done. Or am I wrong?'

'Strict tempo stuff . . . sure.' Again, Hector inhaled cigarette smoke. 'Okay, even that's taken off. But I'm talking about way and gone past that point. I'm talking about something new. And, friend, you hit something new – *really* new – in this rat-race and you're home. By the time the other outfits have worked out a rip-off, you're on the next rung. That way nobody *ever* gets alongside . . . right?'

'The contract said you couldn't,' murmured Pilter.

'Not without Gordon's say-so . . . and Gordon didn't want to know.'

Pilter looked around for something in which to squash out his cigarette. There was a heavy glass ash-tray at one end of the dressing-table and Pilter used it.

As if remarking upon something hardly worthy of mention, he said, 'But Gordon's dead. Cyanide poisoning. Dearden holds a stock of potassium cyanide. And you live with Dearden.'

'Yeah.' Hector scowled at the glowing end of his cigarette.

'The links of a possible chain,' observed Pilter.

'Yeah,' repeated Hector and nodded.

JOHN HECTOR (2)

The ginks of this world, eh? The screwballs who wanted everything dovetailed into place. No untidy corners. No overhang. No pieces that didn't fit.

And yet he, John Hector, didn't fit. No rebel ever did fit and every guy who didn't eat his peas with his fork was, by definition, a rebel.

A musician who played crap, because crap paid the rental. A man – a fully developed man in every other respect – who made love to another man. A man to whom all women were as unimportant as nail-parings.

An untidy corner. Something that didn't fit.

Could be one reason for the cat-and-dog relationship between him and Gordon. The dislike, bordering upon hatred. Gordon . . . one of those guys who was always right, because he was never wrong. The same damn routine. The same bullshit, wrapped up in the same glossy package. And don't disturb the package and don't substitute a little gold for some of the bullshit, otherwise the customers might not play ball and the percentage might drop.

Jesus!

There'd been no way round that contract. No way under it, no way over it, no way through it . . . no way.

Wrong. A quick gargle with potassium cyanide had been a way . . . one way. The only way.

Hence this chinning with a high-powered jack. Hence this buddy-buddy con routine. Hence . . . what else?

'You'll have given it some thought.' Pilter, having squashed out his own cigarette, slid the ashtray towards Hector.

'Yeah.' Hector rolled ash from his cigarette into the ashtray. 'I've – er – y'know . . . decided to send a wreath.'

'Big of you,' observed Pilter gently.

'And a box of cigars to the guy who dumped him.'

'Really?' Pilter smiled. 'I didn't know you smoked cigars.'

'Hey, man!' The sudden blaze of anger in the amazingly blue eyes, died to a twinkle which complimented the slow smile. 'That was low, man.' He screwed out his cigarette, then eased the jockey-shorts around his crotch. 'That was ankle-height, fellah.'

Pilter remained stone-faced as he said, 'You have a temper.'

'Sure,' agreed Hector.

'But?'

'I'm a big boy. I can control it.'

'Nevertheless . . .'

'You may,' interrupted Hector, 'figure me as a lousy musician. That I don't mind, the garbage I play *makes* me a lousy musician. But – friend – don't take me for a dumb bastard. Poison and quick tempers. They don't mix . . . no way.'

'Okay. You're not a dumb bastard,' agreed Pilter.

Hector bobbed his head in acknowledgement of the half-apology.

'So,' added Pilter, 'as a man with brains . . . tell me about Gordon.'

'Sure.' Hector seemed happy – almost anxious – to talk. He said, 'George Gordon. A hard man. Wrong. Wrong in a thousand ways, but always for reasons he thought right. I guess Hitler was wrong for the same reasons.

'No . . .' Hector waved an open hand impatiently. 'No, dammit, that's putting screwy ideas into your head. What he did – everything he did – he figured to be for the best. Everybody's best. He just wouldn't listen. The Big Daddy, see? We were all his kids. We didn't know. We didn't know a damn thing . . . not even when he knew *less*. Y'know . . .' Hector's mouth twisted. 'Some guys give you a real pain. They're always so damn right.'

'I've met the type,' grunted Pilter.

'Okay, that was Gordon. He had this thing about Ray and me. Fixed – y'know . . . Victorian. Edwardian.'

'Non-gay?'

'That in spades.'

'Dearden also has access to potassium cyanide,' said Pilter pointedly.

'For Christ's sake!'

'I know. He wouldn't . . . not in a month of Sundays.'

'He would *not*,' agreed Hector firmly.

'I believe you,' smiled Pilter. 'And Dobson?'

'Y'think *he* might . . .'

'No. Just about him. What makes him tick.'

'He's a skin-basher,' said Hector flippantly. 'After that . . . nothing.'

'He's on pot.'

'Hey, man. You're on that same old wrong highway. From soft drugs to hard drugs, from hard drugs to aggro. It doesn't happen that way.'

'Sometimes,' disagreed Pilter.

'Not with Slam.' Hector wagged an admonishing finger at Pilter. 'I know guys,' he said. 'Slam Dobson. Not the greatest drummer in the world . . . not even if you bury all the other skin-men. The big thing, though . . . eh? No arguments. See? I tell him what I want. Okay, sometimes I have to draw diagrams. It ain't important. Once he gets it, he gets it . . . and it stays.

'Slam . . .' Hector chuckled and scratched the back of his right, naked thigh. He said, 'Slam is scared. All his life. The big talk – the loco weed – it's a cover-up, man. Scared! Every time Gordon *looked* at him he passed blue shit. You talked with him. The night Gordon tipped his hat to the angels, you talked with Slam.'

'We talked,' agreed Pilter.

'A very frightened man . . . right?'

'Mouthy,' grunted Pilter.

'Yeah . . . mouthy. Smokes weed. Dresses like he was a Christmas tree fairy. That's *why*.'

'Because he's scared?'

Hector nodded.

'You could be right,' sighed Pilter. 'Tell him to keep the dope under control.'

'All the time.' Hector grinned. 'I'm one guy he listens to . . . and I tell him that, all the time.'

Pilter chewed at his lower lip for a moment, then murmured, 'Suicide?'

'Eh?' Hector stared.

'Gordon. Would that surprise you?'

'He had that – er – y'know . . . "gentleman's agreement" mentality. The "right thing" . . . sure he'd knock himself off.'

'That's what I think,' lied Pilter heavily.

'So . . . everything's roses?'

'A few thorns. Somebody might still get pricked.'

'Always,' agreed Hector with mock-solemnity. 'Every time you see a rainbow it pisses down.'

I am, thought Pilter, out of my tiny mind. I'm juggling with white-hot cannon balls and, if I drop one, I fry. The killer knows . . . by this time the killer *has* to know. *Has* to have remembered. *Has* to have realised the blinding error. Because – whatever else – the killer is no mug.

The killer . . .

Pilter stared through the windscreen of Baxter's car – stared along the line of the headlights – and found himself saying, 'Suicide. Unofficial as yet, but you might care to pass it round.'

'Y'mean . . .' Baxter turned his head, then jerked his attention back to the road ahead.

'Gordon,' said Pilter.

'In that case, why the hell have we been to . . .'

'I like to see how the other half live.'

Neither spoke for the next quarter of a mile.

Then Baxter said, 'You're having me on.'

124

'No.'

'The inquest was adjourned. It was . . .'

'It'll be re-opened. There'll be a jury. There'll be a verdict. Suicide.'

'Y'mean you can fix these things?'

'Depends how the evidence is presented.'

'Oh!'

Again there was a silence, for about another quarter of a mile.

Then Pilter said, 'Don't you think it *was* suicide?'

'Knowing Gordon . . .'

'You didn't know Gordon,' interrupted Pilter. 'You only *thought* you knew Gordon.'

'Christ!'

'And,' added Pilter wearily, 'I've resigned.'

'Y'mean because . . .'

'Because I'm past retiring age.'

'Oh!'

'I'm tired, Baxter.' Pilter's tone took on a harsh quality. 'I'm getting old and I'm getting tired. I've chased scum a little too long. I don't enjoy it any more.'

'Does that mean Gordon *didn't* . . .'

'It means I don't give a damn any more. That's what it means. That's *all* it means. From now on I want to read about these things in newspapers. That's all . . . that's *all* it means.'

'And – er – it was suicide?'

'Suicide.' Pilter's voice was almost a snarl.

The police squad car was waiting in the drive outside the Baxter farmhouse. It was parked behind Pilter's Rover. As Baxter braked to a halt, two uniformed officers climbed from the front of the squad car and Hulda scrambled from the rear.

For a moment, as Baxter and Pilter opened their respective doors, there was an overlap of voices.

125

'Mr Baxter?'

'Mr Baxter, something terrible has happened.'

'Are you Mr Baxter, sir?'

'I didn't know where you were, Mr Baxter. I couldn't . . .'

'Hold it!' Pilter shouted the small tumult down.

'Who the . . .' One of the patrol officers turned towards Pilter, recognised him and said, 'Sorry, sir. I didn't . . .'

'Forget it. What's happened?'

'Mrs Baxter, sir. And Mrs Gordon. A car accident . . . bad.'

'How bad?' asked Baxter.

'Er – pretty bad, sir. Very bad.'

'For God's sake, man . . .'

'Where?' snapped Pilter.

'Between Gordon's place and here, sir.'

'Fatal?' asked Pilter bluntly.

'I wouldn't be too surprised, sir.' The patrol officer glanced at Baxter, moistened his lips, then said, 'Mrs Baxter was still alive when the ambulance left. Y'know . . . moaning. In a bad way, but still alive.'

'And Mrs Gordon?'

'She was out, sir . . . at least that. Unconscious at least.'

'Possibly dead?'

'I think . . . possibly, sir.'

Hulda was weeping softly. Baxter stood, like a man waiting for a knock-out punch; swaying slightly; panting, as if unable to control his breathing.

Pilter said, 'This is Mr Baxter. Take him to the hospital . . . and wait till there's something definite. Baxter, can I have the keys to this place?'

'Eh?' Baxter blinked some sort of concentration into his eyes.

'The keys. For your house. Miss Deschin can stay here till we've sorted something out . . . we'll all know where everybody is.'

126

'Oh! Sure. Sure.' Baxter fumbled in his pocket, then handed Pilter a key-wallet.

'Right, on your way.'

For a man who, to all intents and purposes, had ended his police career, Pilter was uncommonly active. Having quietened Hulda Deschin enough to have her busy preparing coffee, he used the telephone and, where necessary, pulled rank like the very clappers.

First the Radio Room at Force Headquarters.

He asked for, and was given, all known details of the accident.

'. . . on the way to Baxter's farm. That seems pretty obvious. Mrs Baxter and Mrs Gordon. Mrs Gordon's Mini. From what we can gather, Mrs Gordon was driving and Mrs Baxter was in the front passenger seat. They must have been going at a hell of a lick. The car left the road . . . we think it might have skidded, there's a spot of icing on the surface here and there. Over the grass verge, through a post and rail fence, then down a twelve-foot drop. The car's a complete write-off. The blokes at the scene say Mrs Gordon wasn't wearing a seat-belt. She's a goner . . . nothing official yet, but it seems she left the car through the windscreen. Mrs Baxter was still with us when the ambulance arrived. She was wearing a seat-belt, thank God. Mashed up to hell, but from what the blokes say, mendable.'

'Where's the car?'

'Still at the scene. We've arranged to have it shifted, when the . . .'

'No. Leave it there till I say. Sergeant Jones – the Dabs Section – is he on duty?'

'I think so, sir. I'll check.'

'Do that. And if he's there, get me through to him.'

The familiar clicks and burps peculiar to a telephone switchboard fed themselves into Pilter's ear. Hulda Deschin entered the room carrying a tray holding cups, saucers, a cream jug, a sugar basin and a coffee pot.

'Fine.' Pilter waved his free hand. 'Sit down, girl. Pour . . . black for me and well sweetened. And don't worry. Everything's under control.'

Pilter sipped coffee, until a voice from the telephone earpiece said, 'Sergeant Jones, here.'

'Ah . . . Pilter here, Jones. There's been a road accident. A Mini. Radio Room will give you the location. Can you meet me out there in, say, an hour?'

'Yes, sir.'

'It may be something. It may be a wild goose chase. But, as a personal favour, strict Q.T. I want some prints lifted . . . assuming they're there. But – y'know – nothing on paper. Nothing recorded.'

'I'll be there, sir.'

'It isn't an order, sergeant. Strictly a personal request.'

'I'll be there.'

'Good man.'

Pilter held the prong of the rest down for a moment, then dialled the local hospital.

'There's been a double admission within the last few minutes. A Mrs Baxter and a Mrs Gordon. A road accident. What's their condition?'

'I'm sorry. I can't . . .'

'Who am I talking to?'

'This is the porter's office.'

'Get me somebody with some wool on his back.'

'Look, I'm sorry, but . . .'

'Don't be sorry. Just do as you're told. And *don't* hang up on me, friend. This is Detective Chief Superintendent Pilter talking . . . kill this line and I'll be round there making more trouble than you ever knew existed.'

'I'm sorry, there's nobody . . .'

'There's always *somebody*. Put me through to Casualty.'

'Look, I dunno . . .'

'Put me through to Casualty!'

Pilter sipped coffee as he listened to more blips and buzzes. A woman's voice said, 'Casualty.'

'Detective Chief Superintendent Pilter here. Two recent road accident admissions. A Mrs Baxter and a Mrs Gordon.'

'We're dealing with them at the moment.'

'Fine. What's their condition.'

'I'm sorry. I can't . . .'

'Don't *you* start.'

'What?'

'Apologising. I'm not just being curious. I want some information and I don't want it when *you're* ready.'

'I'll – er – I'll put you onto Sister.'

'Do that.'

There was a silence, then another woman's voice said, 'Sister Neville.'

'Information.' Pilter's growing anger showed in his tone. 'You're handling two casualties at the moment. Road accident. Mrs Baxter and Mrs Gordon. I want . . .'

'I'm afraid I can't . . .'

'Arse me around any more,' roared Pilter, 'and you'll have *cause* to be afraid. The name's Pilter. Detective Chief Superintendent Pilter. And I've already been fobbed off too many times. We – and by "we" I mean the police – need information. We need it *now*. Be advised, lady, give it . . . otherwise you'll find your skirts on fire.'

There was a short spell of heavy breathing then, in a strangled tone, the voice said, 'What – what information?'

'Baxter and Gordon. How are they?'

'Gordon's dead. She was dead on arrival.'

'And Baxter?'

'She has a broken arm. We think she also has a broken pelvis. She's in a very bad condition.'

'Critical?'

'We haven't yet . . .'

'Guess!' snarled Pilter.

'No, I wouldn't say critical. But very badly injured.'

'She'll live?'

'I – I . . .' The voice hesitated, then said, 'Yes. I think she'll live. Other than her injuries, she seems healthy enough. I think she'll live.'

As always, the scene of the accident was a scene of carnage. As always Pilter marvelled that one car – and a Mini at that – could create such havoc. In the lights from the remaining squad car, Jones's parked shooting-brake, the waiting break-down vehicle and Pilter's own Rover, it was all there to see. The dual-carriageway. The scored hard-shoulder. The two curving, gouged-out wounds across the frost-brittle grass of the verge. The shattered and splintered fence. And every-where a scattering of shattered glass and ripped-away metal. The revolving lights on the squad car and the breakdown vehicle – one blue, one yellow – seemed to add visual male-volence to the scene.

'They were going,' observed Jones.

Pilter grunted. He shoved his hands deeper into his mac pockets and walked across the crisp grass to the gaping gap in the post and rail fence.

'Bloody right!' he muttered.

Jones joined him and together they stared down at the wrecked Mini. It was battered well beyond repair; it had obviously turned a complete somersault and landed on its wheels; there was a great dent in the roof and – or so it seemed – it was little more than twisted, smashed-up scrap.

'Anybody walk away from it?' asked Jones.

'No. One dead. One smashed up. This time, *nobody* was lucky.'

They stood in silence for a while, then Jones said, 'What d'you have in mind?'

'Dabs from the steering wheel,' said Pilter softly.

'You'll be lucky!'

'There'll be some. Something. Lift 'em . . . all of 'em.' Pilter took a hand from his pocket and held out a narrow, oblong object, wrapped in a clean handkerchief. He said, 'This, too. It's a watch-case. The watch is inside. If you get a match between prints on the wheel and prints on the box – or on the watch – get me a blow-up. And *exactly* where the print was on the wheel.'

'Will do.' Jones took the proffered parcel.

'Just one thing,' said Pilter. 'The matching doesn't have to go to law . . . there's no court case involved. As long as *we're* satisfied. It's a hunch I have. A personal favour.'

'Sure.' Jones nodded.

Pilter said, 'I'll have the watch back tomorrow. And whatever you can get. But – again a personal favour – don't record this visit. Nothing. Just do it . . . then destroy everything you're not going to give to me.' He turned to look at Jones and added, 'Okay?'

'Okay.' Jones grinned. 'I don't ask silly questions.'

THE DETECTIVE CHIEF SUPERINTENDENT (4)

Thirty-three years. Thirty-three years of hard-nosed bobbying; of punching his way to the top rung of the C.I.D. ladder; of out-facing and out-working flash-style coppers and coming out ahead.

And now this . . .

A real prima-donna act. Something straight from the pages of a Boy's Own Annual.

Thirty-three years for sweet damn-all. To keep a killer's name a secret. To keep a killer on the loose. To tool around with a conscience which, until now, had never stepped between himself and his job. But now – now it had decided to shift itself – that bloody conscience was really digging its talons deep.

To say nothing of Jones.

Okay . . . Jones was a good man; one of the old-fashioned, practical men. A man who, told to hold his peace, would keep his mouth well zipped . . . hopefully! Which was okay . . . but. But that also meant another guy was, albeit unbeknowingly, part of the cover-up. Another guy – a very nice guy – was due for the chop, supposing this crazy game of 'cover-up' ever moved out of its hiding place. It wouldn't of course. It couldn't. The hell! . . . to drop him, to drop Jones, the killer would have to indulge in self-destruction. But – y'know – other people had consciences, too. It had been known.

Consciences were funny bloody things. They tended to up and sing their arias at inopportune moments. They couldn't be relied upon.

Consciences . . .

Thirty-three bloody years and, because of a lot of things, because he'd once had a magnificent evening's entertainment at a London theatre, he suddenly had a runaway conscience. Because of that. Because of a lot of other things, too.

The sealed envelope was on Pilter's desk when he called in at his office the next day. It contained the box and the wristwatch. It also contained two photographs; each a blow-up of a slightly smudged finger mark. Smudged and therefore useless as evidence in a court of law, but good enough for everyday comparison. They were marked 'A' and 'B'. The typed caption clipped to 'A' read 'Right thumb. Inner rim of steering wheel at approximately eleven o'clock'. The typed caption clipped to 'B' read 'Right thumb. Surface of watch face'.

Pilter held the two photographs, one in each hand, and gazed at them. His eyebrows rose fractionally but, despite the confirmation, there was no sign of real pleasure in his eyes. Sadness, perhaps. Sadness, tinged with worry.

He slid the photographs and the cased wrist-watch back into the envelope, then tucked the envelope safely away in his inside breast pocket.

There was a tap on the office door.

Pilter called, 'Come in,' and Skeel entered.

Skeel said, 'It's fixed.'

'What?' For the moment Pilter looked puzzled.

'The re-opened inquest.'

'Oh!'

'Along with his wife,' said Skeel.

'Ah. Yes . . . very appropriate.'

'Close the inquest on both,' said Skeel. 'The coroner seems pleased with the idea.'

'Tidy,' agreed Pilter.

'Will you be there?' asked Skeel.

'No.'

Skeel looked pleased, then straightened his face and said, 'That pile-up last night. Nasty.'

'Very nasty,' agreed Pilter.

'The emotional upset perhaps,' suggested Skeel.

'Possibly.'

'Bound to be.' Skeel spoke as if with authority. 'A woman's husband does himself in. A bad shock. An emotional shock. She shouldn't have been driving.'

Pilter said, 'You could be right.'

'I'm sure of it.' Skeel hesitated then said, 'The – er – the chief constable?'

'What about him?'

'Y'know – you were saying yesterday.'

'A couple of smooth inquests. That should put you right.'

'Ah. Yes . . . of course.'

'Relax a little, Skeel.' Pilter's tone was one of gruff friend-

133

liness. 'He's like you – he's like me – he has bowels and a bladder. He empties 'em, the same way we do.'

'Who?'

'Everybody, including chief constables.'

'Oh!'

'You'll crack,' warned Pilter. 'You're too rigid. Learn to bend a little. Otherwise you'll grow old before your time . . . and you'll crack. Learn to say "Sod 'em" . . . and mean it.'

'I – er – I suppose so.' Skeel gave a watery smile.

'Good advice, Skeel. Best advice I ever offered.'

'Yes – er – thanks. Thanks a lot.' Skeel looked nonplussed. Embarrassed. He walked to the door, then repeated, 'Thanks,' before he left the office.

'Poor bugger,' sighed Pilter . . . and meant it.

'Possible.' Doc Quarmby sucked at his empty pipe to ensure that all the glowing tobacco had been extinguished, thrust the pipe into his jacket pocket, then draped the napkin across his knee before pulling the plate holding the Ploughman's Lunch nearer. He said, 'More than likely, in fact. But forget *locomotor ataxia,* that's out.'

Pilter nodded and tasted his beer.

Doc Quarmby. Pilter's own medic and one of a fast-dying race. A middle-aged man to whom the expression 'family doctor' still had much meaning. To this man his patients were, first and foremost, people; men, women and children to whom disease and pain were twin mysteries. And, to this man, the ripping aside of these mysteries was part of being a medical practitioner.

Over the years Pilter and Quarmby had become far more than doctor and patient. They had become friends and sharers of confidences. They trusted each other completely. And thus Pilter had called in at the public house where Quarmby habitually broke his round-making for lunch in order to pick the medic's brains.

'*Locomotor ataxia.*' Quarmby speared a pickled onion, popped it into his mouth, chewed, swallowed, then waved the fork as he emphasised his point. 'A foul disease, Tom. I wouldn't wish it on my worst enemy. Nothing sudden . . . and that's what you're on about. Nothing sudden about *locomotor ataxia*. Starts off with shooting pains. Then the jerking starts. It can be controlled – more or less – with drugs. Sometimes – very rarely – an operation can sort things out. But when the thing really gets hold, the poor devil flaps away like a stranded fish. Can't help himself. And an invalid chair isn't too much help. More often than not he has to be strapped in . . . otherwise he'd jerk himself out of the damn thing.'

'He couldn't pour himself a drink,' mused Pilter.

'Not a hope in hell.' Doc Quarmby sliced a sliver of cheese, fed it into his mouth, then tore the bread bun and plastered it with butter. 'Forget *locomotor ataxia*,' he said. 'Your hypothetical invalid isn't cursed with *that* ailment.'

'Hemiplegia?' suggested Pilter.

Quarmby said, 'The brain goes on the blink.' He chewed buttered bread, swallowed, then downed a quarter of a pint in one swallow. 'Old hacks like me call it a "stroke". Sometimes serious, sometimes only temporary. Something clobbers one side of the brain. Usually something inside. A blood vessel ruptures . . . summat like that. The left side of the brain takes the thump, the right side of the body takes the paralysis. It works that way. Left side of the brain, right side of the body. Right side of the brain, left side of the body. There's a cross-over.'

'An accident?' fished Pilter.

'Not usually.' He popped cheese into his mouth. 'Not impossible, but it's usually an internal thing.'

'And a wheelchair?'

'No.' Quarmby shook his head. 'Bed. Rest. Bags of quiet. A man gets clobbered with hemiplegia, he stays in bed until

135

he can walk. If he can get out of bed – if he can walk . . . he's just about cured.'

Quarmby munched away at his pub lunch. He paused periodically to swill his mouth clean with a long draughts of beer. His concentration – or so it seemed – was focused upon eating and drinking. He seemed to be untouched by the rise and fall of background chatter from the other customers. Indeed, he seemed unaware of the presence of Pilter; as if having had his questions answered, Pilter had left and he Quarmby was being allowed to enjoy a solitary meal in peace.

Pilter went along with the make-believe. He remained silent until he'd finished his own beer, then left the table for the bar and returned with two newly-pulled pints.

'Thanks.' Quarmby acknowledged Pilter's existence.

Pilter tasted his own beer, then said, 'Okay . . . paraplegia?'

'Where the hell,' grumbled Quarmby, 'do you get all these fancy ailments?'

'Glaister's. It's a . . .'

'I know what Glaister wrote. Medical jurisprudence. Toxicology. A damn good book. But . . .'

'Paraplegia?' insisted Pilter.

'From Glaister's angle?'

'Obviously.'

'Right.' Quarmby drank beer then again used his fork as a form of pointer with which to emphasise his remarks. 'Paraplegia has to do with the spinal cord . . . right? Goof *that* one up and you're in trouble. Everything below the injury – below the disease – stops functioning. Basics . . . not enough blood supply to the cord, syphilis, falling and smacking the spine. All these things – and more – can cause it. Some quacks still hang on to the theory that too much masturbation can bring it on, but that's so much balls. Start on that road and you end up by believing that a man can

136

shag himself into a paraplegic . . . and that's real market-square medicine. But if it's a fall – say – it can often be cured. Somebody with a broken spine. Temporary paraplegia. A foul condition, but it could be worse . . . he could be dead. And as the spine mends – as the spinal cord gets working again – he's as good as new. Except . . .

'Except,' continued Quarmby softly, 'very often he *ain't* as good as new. With a man, especially. The old procreative organs . . . they stay on the knock. The bit that's politely known as "the genitals". It doesn't do its stuff any more. The lad stays impotent. No erection. No nothing. Everything else as it should be, but the old pecker won't stiffen.' He raised his eyebrows and ended, 'Anything else?'

'Yes. That . . .' Pilter nodded at the almost-empty plate, 'is on me.'

And the days grew into weeks and the weeks grew into months and Pilter was no longer a police officer.

There was the usual booze-up shambles on the day he officially handed in his warrant card; men who had previously hardly hidden their dislike of him, thumped him on the back and told him what a bloody good bloke he was; the 'going away' present was the usual clock, handed over with the usual platitudes and accepted with the usual empty-worded crap . . . and everybody, including Pilter, knew damn well it was all moonshine.

The two inquests on George and Ruth Gordon were re-opened, held and closed – 'Suicide' and 'Death by Misadventure' – and the two coffins followed each other into the crematorium furnace.

Meanwhile Thomas Pilter learned to live with his retirement.

Nor was that as easy as he had at first thought.

Coppering – even the high-altitude coppering of Pilter's last few years – was no routine job; no fixed hours, no fixed meal-times, no pattern via which the body might set its own alarm clock. The choice of 'rut', therefore, was the first hurdle. And, because he was unmarried, Pilter had no wife with a ready-made domestic discipline into which he might fit his own life. Trial and error was required before he fathomed the best way in which he might pass his days.

He discovered, somewhat to his surprise, that 'early nights' were out. Sleep came at about one o'clock in the morning and this irregardless of the time he went to bed. The evenings, therefore, were spent watching what few good programmes the television had to offer and reading books he'd always *meant* to read. Thus (for the first time in his life) he became conscious of T.V. playwrights; Potter, Bennet and the small stable of fellow-experts whose dialogues and ideas were a guarantee of good viewing. He also discovered – and sometimes re-discovered – the delights of Steinbeck, Hemingway, and men (and a few women) who penned fiction based upon their own experiences of life.

From an increased interest in T.V. was born an increased interest in radio, and from an increased interest in radio was born an increased interest – an increased awareness – of good music. He was too long in the tooth for experimentation with the modern composers, but the magnificence of the masters left him bright-eyed and choking.

The tempo of his life slackened. The subconscious nervous tension, which is a by-product of an accumulation of non-stop policing, gradually eased and, as a result, he became a more tranquil person.

Occasionally, he visited the live theatre, grew to enjoy it and, after about a year of retirement, took the plunge and tried his first taste of live grand opera.

FLASHBACK

Saturday, April 1st, 1966. Half a world away it was All Fools Day but in Adelaide it was the last day of an Australian-New Zealand tour which had taken in Christchurch, Napier, Auckland, Sydney, Brisbane, Melbourne, Perth and now Adelaide. A great tour; one of those tours stage people talk about, but rarely experience. For two months The Great Gordano and Company had played to packed houses; critics and public alike had raved about the slick, non-stop presentation of illusions, each of which could of itself have been the climax of any normal stage magician's act. Nightly 'impossibilities' had been commonplace. Lesser illusionists had come to watch . . . and left mystified. Already negotiations were under way for a return tour in three years' time.

But first – and the next planned triumph – was a season at the London Coliseum.

Gordano was on the empty stage of the theatre, explaining to his two principal assistants – his wife, Ruth, and the man who had replaced Herman Deschin, Jim Fairbanks – the illusion to end all illusions.

'The Disappearing Audience,' he said. 'With a full season at one theatre – the Coliseum – it can be done. We need a full season, though. Otherwise, the cost defeats the whole object.'

Fairbanks said, 'Okay . . . tell us how.'

'Out there.' Gordano waved his arms towards the empty

139

auditorium. 'A full house. Up here.' He turned and backed towards the stage apron. 'A mirror. Glass. It has to be glass, because it's a two-way mirror. Slightly convex. It has to be convex, in order that every member of the audience can see himself. Herself. It will also give a slight distortion . . . a point in our favour, in case of minor slip-ups. Let the mirror down from the flies.' Gordano tilted his head and continued to wave his arms. 'That's your job, Jim. A mirror with a black, light-proof, velvet surround. Lowered to an *exact* spot.

'The house-lights are turned on. Everybody sees a genuine reflection of the body of the theatre. An audience distraction – at the moment I'm in favour of a cannon shot. Blank, of course. From the back of the theatre . . . that should take their eyes away from the stage for a split second.

'That's when I want a back-projection still of the empty theatre – as seen from the stage – thrown onto the reverse side of the two-way mirror. Done properly, it should kill the image and what they'll see is rows and rows of empty seats. A vanished audience, in fact.

'I know.' Gordano's enthusiasm bubbled over. 'Snags . . . snags galore. It must be a damn good photograph. The best we can get. *And* taken through a curved lense. But some gimmicks might help. A bulb out – say – on one of the chandeliers. Looks like an accident, but it isn't. The same "dud" bulb comes up on the picture. An odd empty seat here and there . . . deliberately empty. Show them in the picture, too. Get a good photographer. The best we can find. Half a dozen shots. Each with its own "proof" – something the audience will latch onto – that the reflection is real.

'It needs working on. I know it needs working on. The timing, the positioning . . . everything has to be perfect. But it can be done. The greatest illusion, *ever*!' Gordano laughed aloud as his enthusiasm bubbled over and gave voice. 'Audience participation as never before. We need to be careful . . . that's all. Just the three of us. Jim to lower the mirror.

You, Ruth, to be ready to throw the image onto the back of the mirror, just when the cannon shot distracts everybody. The right patter. A slight variation of the various gimmicks each performance. Everybody else out of the way. Out of the wings. Off the catwalks. This is *our* illusion. The finale of the first half . . . the safety curtain lowers on a reflection of an empty theatre. Yes, I think that. I think that might be the cherry on top of the cake. Snags? Of course there'll be snags. The lighting has to be perfect. The photography, the timing . . . everything perfect. It's a price, but when we've paid it . . .'

He was backing away, arms wide, head tilted as he gazed up at the ropes and limes, high above the stage. Ruth Gordon's cry of warning came fractionally too late. His left heel caught against the edge of the footlight shield, his arms windmilled and he sprawled backwards into the orchestra pit and, as the edge of the piano smashed into his spine, the echoes of his scream seemed to bounce from wall to wall of the empty theatre.

The Australian medics saved his life; for a few days it was touch and go because of the unskilled First Aid given by his wife and Fairbanks. A broken back is no small matter and a broken back, aggravated by people anxious to make the sufferer 'comfortable' prior to the arrival of an ambulance, can be fatal.

Simple economics demanded that The Gordano Company be disbanded. The decision was, nevertheless, postponed until Gordon himself could *make* that decision from a hospital bed. Other than his wife every member of the company was handed a first-class ticket back to England plus three months' salary. They were all promised as much help as Gordon could give in their search for other employment.

It was quite a ceremony and, when the last of them had left the tiny, well-equipped ward of the private nursing home,

Ruth said, 'They'll miss you, George. You're really rather unique, you know.'

'The Disappearing Audience.' Gordon's voice was not without bitterness. 'The Great Gordano . . . *he's* the one that's disappeared.'

'Please! Have a little faith.'

Gordon's mouth twisted and he said, 'The Australian medical profession don't believe in mincing words. They've warned me. I might never walk again.'

'Which, in turn, means you *might.*'

'I prefer to be a pessimist. They're never disappointed.'

'*I* prefer to be an optimist.'

She lighted two cigarettes, handed one to him and they smoked in silence for a few minutes.

Then Gordon said, 'Hulda.'

'What about her?'

'No father. Not even me any more.'

'Of course she has you. You've been a second father to her since . . .'

'People have their pride, Ruth.'

'I don't see what that has . . .'

'When I get out of here, I'll need a nurse. I'll need Hulda.'

'You're going to walk again,' she insisted.

He smiled and said, 'I'll need a nurse. I'll need Hulda.'

'Yes, dear. When we get home.'

That (although neither of them recognised it as such) was their first clash of wills. The first tiny rebellion within the until then tranquillity of their married life. And, moreover, a victory – or, at least, a half-victory – for Ruth Gordon.

Seven months later Gordon was in an invalid chair, and they were sailing for the United Kingdom.

From the limelight to obscurity. The metamorphosis was complete. They landed in England as Mr and Mrs Gordon; the press and public were already well on the way to forgetting The Great Gordano. They were met at the dock by

142

Ruth's sister, Celia, and the man she'd married, Neil Baxter ... nobody else. The crates of magical equipment – the wherewithal via which Gordon had amazed audiences around the world – were sealed and stored, pending some other would-be-wizard buying their secrets. Miracles for sale. A life's collection of 'impossibilities' there for the purchase.

If Gordon was bitter, he tried to hide it, and consoled himself with the undoubted fact that he was a very rich man. Call it 'an early retirement' – call it any name under the sun – the fact remained, he had not quite reached the summit he'd set himself. The best in the world . . . yes. The best of his own generation . . . yes. But the best *ever* . . . perhaps yes, but perhaps no. The close-knit fraternity of stage magicians would agree. Houdini, Maskelyne, Devant, Chung Ling Soo, Dante, Gordano. Which *had* been the greatest? The arguments would still continue. But Gordon's driving ambition had always been to make all arguments centre around the *second*-best.

But who could manipulate illusions from a wheelchair?

They'd found the house of their final choice, tucked away in a fold of the Yorkshire Dales. A mini-mansion which, with first-class central heating, double-glazing, widened doors to take the wheelchair, the installation of a lift and other, lesser, alterations became – for Gordon – an ideal and luxurious prison in which he might work the self-pity from his system.

It was a slow and painful process. Man is an animal; a pack animal, according to the experts. And, as in a pack, when one of the pack's number becomes sick or injured the healthy members of the pack ignore it and leave it to die or, alternatively, savage it to a quicker death in order that it might not hinder or obstruct the progress and efficiency of the close community of the pack itself. Thus goes the argument. And from this argument stems the natural embarrassment of the healthy when confronted by the diseased or the incomplete; sympathy, by the laws of nature, is 'unnatural' . . . and the veneer of civilisation upon which that sympathy rests is rarely more than paper-thin. Give a man crutches and he becomes an affront to all manhood. Put a man in a wheelchair and the chair becomes, symbolically, far more important than the man himself.

Every man – every woman – who, for whatever cause, is confronted with this backlash of primeval (albeit unconscious and hidden) attitude becomes embittered. In some the bitterness lasts a lifetime. But in others the personality change is such that, gradually, the man comes to dominate the crutches – to dominate the wheelchair – and from that moment he (or she) is *genuinely* accepted as a fully-paid-up-member of mankind. Once more he is vital to 'the pack' . . . and acknowledged as such.

Gradually – very gradually – Gordon fought the wheelchair and, eventually, conquered it. The pitch and toss of argument no longer disgusted him; instinct told him that those with whom he argued no longer counted his infirmity as a weakness which, even in the heat of disagreement, they must respect.

And his relationship with his wife?

He was her 'husband' in name only. This saddened him and, in the privacy of his own thoughts, haunted him with a feeling of shame and inadequacy. For the first time in his life he was forced to accept the proposition of 'impossible'. He who in the past had almost off-handedly performed 'miracles', was forced to the realisation that he couldn't even accomplish an act which other grown men took for granted.

As a form of compensation he denied his wife nothing. Nothing! Whatever she wished – whatever whim took her fancy – that was enough for him. He elevated her to the status of goddess . . . and, as such, worshipped her.

His basic mistake?

144

In believing that the act of worship could ever be a sufficient substitute for love.

Nevertheless, the bitterness left him. His mind opened itself to new ideas. He gathered around himself friends and acquaintances – men and women from the world of the theatre – men and women who had known him in his days of greatness . . . men and women who now toured the 'club circuits' and who convinced him that there was still room at the top.

Nine years after his fall from the stage of the Adelaide theatre, he put the proposition to his brother-in-law, Neil Baxter. They were alone at the time – Ruth and Celia were out at some local fashion-show or another – and (although Baxter never guessed the reason) Gordon chose his brother-in-law because he was married to Ruth's sister.

Gordon said, 'Neil, I have this scheme.'

'What scheme?' Baxter turned from the window; from gazing out at the rise and fall of the surrounding countryside.

'There's room for an agency.'

'An agency?' Baxter frowned non-understanding. The truth was he wasn't too damn keen on this crippled brother-in-law of his. A man can't walk – a man has to move around on wheels – that man ought not to be so damn sure of himself. Baxter said, 'What sort of an agency?'

'Theatrical.'

'For Christ's sake! They're ten-a-penny. London's . . .'

'The northern club-circuit,' interrupted Gordon.

Baxter strolled towards the tiny, well-stocked bar and sneered, 'Chicken-feed.'

'They're hungry for acts . . . good acts.'

As he poured himself whisky-and-water Baxter said, 'Maybe.'

'I *know.*'

'So?'

'I have the contacts.'

'George, you're kidding yourself. Those places work on a shoe-string. They pay peanuts. They ...'

'They have the money. They pay more money than the old-timers ever knew existed.'

'Okay.' Baxter sipped his drink and conceded a point. 'The big clubs. The plush places. But ...'

'And they're hungry for good acts.'

'Sure.' Once more Baxter conceded a point. 'But where are the good acts who don't yet *have* agents?'

'The semi-pro crowd, Neil.'

'Oh, for God's sake!'

'The pickings are good.'

'With semi-pro crap?'

'I know talent when I see it. *I'll* audition.'

Some of the enthusiasm sparked across to Baxter. Gordon – and nobody could argue against *that* proposition – knew show-biz. In the past he'd topped too many bills for there to be any doubt upon that point. Baxter sipped his drink and allowed himself to be won over.

Gordon said, 'All I need is somebody capable of taking care of the cash side of things.'

'An accountant. Like me?'

Gordon nodded and said, 'Somebody to visit the concert secretaries.'

'That easy?' Baxter pulled a face. 'We need an "in", George. Everybody needs an "in" . . . if he's going to get anywhere.'

'My name still means something. My guarantee carries weight.'

'Could be.' Baxter sounded doubtful. 'But with semi-pro . . .'

'Good acts. Polished acts. I'll find them. You sell them.'

'Among the semi-pro crowd?'

'They all want to turn pro. I'll *make* them professionals. I'll show them *how*.' Gordon, despite the restriction of the

146

wheelchair, still had the habit of waving his arms when enthusing. He waved them now. 'They'll sell their souls . . . their souls!'

'Okay.' Baxter's mind slipped into gear, added, subtracted, divided and multiplied; the paths and by-lanes leading to a dozen rip-offs brought him in line with Gordon's own zeal. He said, 'Where do we start? How?'

'Find a solicitor,' said Gordon.

'What?'

'I want a contract. Air-tight, water-tight, bomb-proof.'

'Okay.' Baxter nodded. 'As long as they'll sign.'

'They'll sign. All *you* have to do is sell.'

And Gordon was as good as his word. He used the hard-headed professionals he'd once worked with as his scouts. Without once moving from his home he heard of talent other agencies had overlooked. He arranged auditions. He listened, he watched, he advised. Then, once the contract had been signed, he polished and every time the end-product had that sheen – that extra sparkle – the clubs were howling for. His stand-up comics were made to discard their outrageous clothes; they were made to wear tailored dinner-suits, hand-made shirts and immaculate bow-ties; they were made to *look* good, before they even opened their mouths; they were taught timing – how to gauge an audience via the reaction to the first gag – how to pace their patter and wait for the laughs; how to enter and (even more important) how to exit. His duo turns were equally moulded into comic and feed; they were introduced to the secret of the running-gag; they were taught how to get laughs via facial expression, without facial distortion; it was explained to them that no great double-act had included a tap routine, but that many had introduced the soft-shoe exit . . . because (for some mysterious reason) a soft-shoe exit 'fitted' a good comic-and-feed spot.

All his adult life Gordon had worked within smelling distance of grease paint. His forte had been stage magic but at

147

the same time he had rubbed shoulders with the 'greats' of the entertainment world. Like a dry sponge he'd soaked up the mysteries of their success. Every type of act ever to reach top-billing . . . as if by instinct Gordon knew why *that* act had shouldered aside all similar acts.

Even the strippers.

'Look, lady . . . you're not there just to take your clothes off. Every married man in the audience – and a lot of unmarried men – see a woman take her clothes off every night. They're not paying for *that*. They're paying for something different . . . and not just a different woman. Make it pornographic and every woman in the audience will hate you. But make it *erotic* . . . they'll all applaud. You're not getting into a bath. You're not getting ready for bed. You're an artist. Remember that. Every movement – every movement of the head, every movement of the body, every movement of the hand or the fingers, every movement of the foot or the toes . . . they're *all* practised and deliberate. Slow. *Very* slow. In tempo with the music, but at half that tempo. The music is rasping and brash. Make it a contrast. *You* be seductive and shy. And I mean shy . . . not arsing around doing a hard-to-get routine. You understand what I mean? If not . . . on your way.'

That brand of ruthless perfectionism rocketed The Gordon Agency to the top. Baxter no longer had to travel the circuit, coaxing the concert secretaries. Instead, the concert secretaries telephoned the agency and begged for more acts.

And because success spawns success, not a few of the already-established acts added their names to the books of this agency of 'the best'.

The rebel act was The Ectoplasm.

John Hector was no starry-eyed young hopeful ready to accept, without complaint or argument, Gordon's every instruction. Hector knew his own worth and, moreover, also knew that, even without The Gordon Agency, his group could

148

eventually have topped most other groups. Indeed, as time went by, Hector began to form a firm opinion; that, far from helping The Ectoplasm in their fight for peak place, Gordon was holding them back. Gordon, it seemed, knew many things – knew *most* things, about theatrical presentation . . . but knew damn-all about music.

'We need a tenor sax,' said Hector.

'Why?'

The two of them were alone, in the tiny office Gordon used as a hub from which he controlled the agency. Gordon's wheelchair was at the table-desk. Hector lounged in the armchair.

Hector said, 'A different sound. A better sound.'

'A tenor saxophone?'

'Yeah.'

'I don't agree.'

'I didn't think you would.' Hector's reply carried sarcastic overtones.

'You're doing well,' said Gordon.

'We could be doing better.'

'With a tenor saxophone?' This time Gordon's voice held sarcasm.

Hector said, 'We play the same sort of crap every other group plays. We play it a little better . . . that's the only difference.'

'That . . . and the salary.'

'To say nothing of the percentage.'

'I'm not the one who's grumbling.'

'Look.' Hector held his anger in check. 'Every outfit that ever made musical history did it with a new sound. Since jazz started . . . okay? Whiteman, Miller, Last, The Beatles, The Stones, The Swingle . . . they were all *different*. They all broke new ground.'

'Now you want to make musical history?'

'Put that way . . . yeah.'

149

'Not money?'

'The difference *makes* the money.'

'Polish makes the money, Hector. Polish, plus presentation ... haven't you learned *that* yet?'

'Gordon, this is my group,' said Hector coldly.

'*Our* group.'

'The hell!'

'Check the contract ... *our* group.'

'That damn contract ...'

'You signed it.'

'That was one hell of a bad day for me.'

'You didn't think so at the time.'

Hector took a deep breath then said, 'I need a tenor sax, Gordon. I need counter-melody. Depth. Something I can build new arrangements on.'

'I know what you mean by "new arrangements".'

'So?'

'That's out.'

'For Christ's sake!'

'No "new arrangements",' snapped Gordon. 'Pop groups and classical music don't mix. Nobody's *really* satisfied. You have an audience. A following. Be satisfied. Build on it. No tenor saxophones. No "new arrangements". End of argument. Find your own way out ... I'm busy.'

It wasn't the first row. It wasn't the last. Both men believed themselves to be right, and probably both men *were* right. Despite the abruptness of his manner, Gordon recognised real musicianship in Hector. But, damn it, it was a group. It wasn't the London Symphony Orchestra. It had to be held on a tight rein, otherwise all the headway might be flushed down the drain for the sake of a gamble. And The Gordon Agency didn't gamble. It backed winners ... every time. And that the winners might be only a neck ahead made them no less winners. Hector wanted the field to himself ... and George wouldn't give him it.

150

The Ectoplasm. The running sore of the agency. Everything ended up with The Ectoplasm. The relationship between Hector and the photographer, Dearden. The doubtful drumming ability of the dressed-up oaf, Dobson. *Everything* ended up with The Ectoplasm.

But . . . what the hell?

Every agency had its wildcat problems.

And it *was* a fine agency . . . and as the years passed it became better.

FINAL SCRUTINY

En toute chose il faut considérer la fin.
In all matters one must consider the end.

Le Renard et le Bouc
Jean De La Fontaine

The bustle and chatter in the foyer was evidence of the standard of the performance. Pilter hadn't understood a word, but the obvious French-farce plot, coupled with Mozart's bubbling music, had sufficed. *The Marriage of Figaro* had been his first opera. It wasn't going to be his last. He waited patiently to collect his overcoat and hat from the cloakroom and in his mind the melodies still tumbled and turned.

A voice at his elbow said, 'A good production.'

'What?' Pilter turned.

'A good production,' repeated Baxter. He added, 'I didn't know you were an opera buff.'

'I'm not.' Pilter smiled. 'This is my first taste.'

'And?'

'A night to remember.'

'I think so, too. It's a pity they don't tour the provinces more often.'

It was small-talk as they edged their way nearer to the cloakroom counter. Small-talk, but with a subtle difference.

Baxter said, 'I read of your retirement.'

'Yes.'

'A bit of a surprise.'

'Was it?'

'Y'know . . .' Baxter moved a shoulder. 'Chief superintendents. Detective chief superintendents. Nobody thinks they *will* retire.'

'They all do . . . eventually,' Pilter assured him.

'Your wife'll be pleased.' Baxter turned his head. 'Is she here?'

'It's a luxury I've never indulged in.'

'An old bachelor?'

' 'Fraid so.' Pilter grinned.

Small-talk, but with a subtle difference. Baxter was more relaxed; less haughty, less complacent. A better man – a more friendly man – and it showed in his speech and in his manner.

Pilter said, 'Your wife?'

'She's around somewhere.' Baxter craned his neck. 'Collecting her coat. Powdering her nose.'

'She recovered from the accident?'

'Oh, yes.' Baxter was suddenly sombre. 'God . . . I nearly lost her that time.'

They reached the counter together, handed in their tickets and waited.

Baxter said, 'Are you going home to an empty house then?'

'Usage.' Pilter took his coat and hat from the attendant. 'I'm pretty organised.'

As if on an impulse Baxter said, 'End the evening at our place.'

'Good Lord, it's miles out.'

'Please.' Baxter seemed suddenly eager. 'A chat. A drink. Celia would be delighted. And there's a cold buffet waiting . . . plenty of it.'

Pilter hesitated.

Baxter took his clothes from the attendant, glanced over the heads of the crowd and called 'Darling!' He waved a hand, then turned to Pilter and said, 'Please . . . as a favour.'

'If – er – if your wife wouldn't mind.'

'We've been going to ask you.'

And Pilter had the distinct impression that the remark was not an empty politeness. This man, Baxter, really *had* changed. It was as if that which had once made him obnoxious had been remove from his personality; as if he'd

156

grown in stature and, in doing so, had become a more complete – a more understanding – man.

Celia Baxter, too, had changed. The vivacity was still there, as was the poise, but now it was real whereas before it had been a put-on. Her laughter was spontaneous. Her wit was no longer snide; no longer barbed and cruel. Furthermore, she had periods of seriousness; periods in which Pilter realised that she was both well-read and compassionate.

He was glad he'd accepted Baxter's invitation.

They'd eaten chicken sandwiches and mushroom patties. They'd enjoyed freshly percolated coffee. And now – at almost midnight – they were all three relaxed in armchairs, sipping sherry and smoking cigarettes. The room was warm and comfortable. The talk had been stimulating. Nobody was willing to break the spell of companionship.

'How's the agency?' asked Pilter.

'Finished,' said Baxter.

'Really?' Pilter sounded surprised.

'It wasn't my agency. It was Gordon's . . . all Gordon's.'

'I had the impression you were a partner.'

'No. An employee . . . that's all. We've expanded the farm. That's enough to keep us in moderate luxury.'

'I see.'

There was a silence of perhaps thirty seconds, then Celia Baxter said, 'What did you think of my brother-in-law, Mr Pilter?'

'I – er – I didn't know him,' fenced Pilter.

'You asked questions.'

'Of course. That was necessary.'

'And the picture?'

'Of George Gordon?'

'Yes.' She nodded. 'Of my brother-in-law. What conclusions did you reach?'

'A perfectionist.' Pilter chose his words with great care

He sipped at the sherry, then continued, 'The Great Gordano. I once saw him. Years ago. Like tonight's opera. An evening not to forget.'

'George Gordon,' she insisted gently.

'I think . . .' Pilter paused, again sipped his sherry, then said, 'A one-off job. Some of his illusions were fabulous. They've never been repeated. They've never been equalled. At a guess I'd say that was a pointer. Somebody – I won't say who – called him "dictatorial", then withdrew the remark and substituted "despotic". I can understand that. To be in charge of an act, as involved and as gigantic as his was, must have called for certain qualities.'

'Always being right?' she suggested gently.

'No.' Pilter shook his head. 'Being able to make a decision.'

She smiled knowingly.

'As I understand it,' said Pilter, 'he treated all his employees . . . well.'

'Oh, yes.'

'That, at least, in his favour. Some people don't.'

'As The Great Gordano,' she murmured.

Baxter added, 'As George Gordon he was something of a martinet. That contract was like a straitjacket.'

'I've been told,' said Pilter.

Celia Baxter leaned forward in her chair and said, 'Mr Pilter. Three civilians . . . right? Not a policeman in sight. Not a policeman within earshot. Shall I tell you what George Gordon – The Great Gordano – was *really* like?'

'It might be interesting.'

'Well, now. Until his accident – he had an accident in Adelaide, you know that?'

'I've heard. Since the enquiry.'

'Only since the enquiry?'

'Let's say I suspected something of the sort towards the end of the enquiry.'

'Let's say that,' she agreed. 'Before his accident he was a

158

magician. One of the best . . . perhaps *the* best. Magicians? Odd people . . . that's an opinion I've reached. Think about it. Stage magic is a facsimile of the real thing. That's all it is. A "pretence" of magic. But with a man like George Gordon . . . I wonder. His "pretence" was so good. Logic insists that he must have considered – at the very least *considered* – the possibility of that extra step. A step into the darkness. Merlin's territory.'

Pilter said, 'The nurse, Hulda Deschin, hinted at things.'

'Of course. Her father was a stage magician . . . he, too, must have toyed with the possibility.'

'It's ridiculous,' grunted Pilter.

'Of course it's ridiculous,' she agreed gently. 'To we three here in this room it's ridiculous. Utterly ridiculous. But for the sake of argument accept an assumption. That you – personally – can fake magic . . . fake it as expertly as George Gordon once could. Then accept the argument *he* must have accepted. The real thing. Never proved . . . but never *dis*proved. There *are* things we know little about, Mr Pilter. In Africa. In the Far East. On the Indian Continent. Things we can't fully explain.

'Accept that – that assumption, that argument – and the rest follows. George Gordon was curious. He *had* to be curious. So near, but *how* near?'

'The Indian Rope Trick,' murmured Pilter.

'One puzzle,' she agreed. 'One of many. One of thousands. And a man like George Gordon – a perfectionist – had to know.'

'Y'mean, he dabbled in the occult?'

'No.' She shook her head. Then she smiled and continued, 'To be honest, I don't know, he may have done. But for now let's say "No". It wasn't necessary. Just to believe – to half believe – not to *dis*believe would have been enough. A form of madness . . . surely? A special form of madness. A mad-

159

ness capable of making a man see himself almost as a God. Superior.'

Pilter said, 'Master of his own destiny.'

'Of course.'

'Somebody said that, too.'

'That,' she said, 'was only part of it. It was deeper than that. Bigger than that. More terrifying.' She paused, sipped sherry, then drew on her cigarette and continued, 'Mr Pilter, I once thought I knew men. I once really *thought* that. When Ruth married Gordon I was happy. This man – this George Gordon – would be more than a husband. He'd protect her . . . *really* protect her. A sort of father-cum-husband figure. I truly believed that. I was happy for her.'

'And you were wrong?'

She nodded.

Quietly, but very deliberately, Pilter said, 'Because you didn't know Gordon? Or because you didn't know your sister?'

Baxter cleared his throat and said, 'I think we'd do well to change the subject.'

'No!' Celia Baxter raised her glass to eye level – as if in a toast – and said. 'Mr Pilter, I think you earned the rank of detective chief superintendent.'

'I'm no longer in the force,' he reminded her.

'Why?'

'I retired.'

'Why?'

'I was past retiring age. Other men wanted my job.'

'No.' She shook her head gently. 'I mean *why*? Why at that particular moment?'

'Because . . .' He floundered and seemed unable to continue.

'Because you knew too much,' she said softly.

'I knew enough,' he admitted. 'Enough, but *not* enough.'

'Tell me,' she invited.

Baxter said, 'Darling, I think you're prying. I think . . .'

'Please.' She kept her eyes on Pilter and ignored Baxter's remark.

'All right.' Pilter cleared his throat. 'You've already said. Three of us. Not a policeman in sight. You know . . . maybe you *both* know.'

'We both know,' said Baxter solemnly.

'So, as an exercise. To prove something. If only that all coppers aren't dumb.'

'First a re-fill.' Baxter seemed to have resigned himself to the inevitable. He stood up from his chair, topped all three glasses from a decanter, then returned to the chair. 'Now, your conclusions, Mr Pilter.'

'Facts. First of all, facts.' Pilter squashed his cigarette into a stand ashtray. 'The first fact. The first *obvious* fact that pointed my nose in the right direction. A matter of tears. A matter of weeping. George Gordon. Poisoned. Bang – just like that . . . and nobody – *nobody* shed a tear. Shock? Sure there was shock all right. But the wrong sort of shock. The shock you might get at a road accident. But his wife – his sister-in-law, his brother-in-law . . . no sorrow. A strange man. A peculiarly unloved man.'

'An unpopular man,' murmured the woman.

'Maybe.' Pilter nodded slowly. 'Unpopular, but unpopular *despite* all he did. From what I can gather he didn't go out of his way to be unpopular. Just – y'know – something about him. Some men are built that way. The capacity to be loved isn't in 'em. They don't know why. Nobody knows why. It's just missing. They end up like Gordon. Unhappy. Inside – unhappy – frustrated. Even those who *should* love 'em, don't.'

'Clever,' breathed the woman.

'Sad,' contradicted Pilter. 'A man who wants to love – who wants to *be* loved – but lacks that quality, is a man to be pitied. Maybe – here I'm guessing – maybe he thought he could *buy* love. Maybe he thought he could *earn* love by

161

taking on the role of protector. With you . . .' Pilter glanced at Baxter. 'By giving you a life-style you'd never dared dream about. By taking over the responsibility of Hulda Deschin. All these things.' Pilter sighed. 'He wasn't even popular.'

Baxter said, 'He didn't want to be popular.'

'But he wanted to be loved?'

'Yeah.' Baxter nodded. 'That . . . perhaps.'

Celia Baxter said, 'He trusted nobody. That was one of his big faults. He trusted nobody.'

'In his world?' said Pilter. 'Where illusions are filched whenever possible? Agreed, he trusted nobody. That was part of the price he had to pay for being The Great Gordano. That and the fact that his world was a close-knit, make-believe world.'

'He was always right,' growled Baxter. 'Always!'

Pilter smiled and said, 'A spin-off. Despots don't go in for a show of hands. But – basically – he lacked love. He didn't even know its real meaning.'

'And yet,' said the woman slowly, 'not a bad man. That to his credit. Not a *bad* man.'

'Incomplete,' Pilter said. 'We come across 'em. In the force . . . men who hurt, without meaning to hurt. Without even *knowing* they're hurting.'

'No policemen present,' Baxter reminded him.

'Point taken.' Pilter grinned, tasted his sherry, then spoke to the woman. 'To solve a murder, Mrs Baxter . . .'

'Murder?' She presented surprise.

'To solve a murder,' he insisted gently. 'It sometimes becomes necessary to understand the personality of the victim. George Gordon. Once The Great Gordano. A king unthroned because of an accident in Adelaide in – when was it? – 1966. It could have killed him. At a guess I think he sometimes wished it had. Paralysed from the waist down. Anchored to a wheelchair . . .'

162

'That damn wheelchair,' began Baxter. 'According to the inquest . . .'

'Unnecessary.' Pilter nodded. 'But not at first. The spine mended. The injury mended . . . gradually. When? We'll never know. Was his wife aware of its mending? Again we'll never know, but I think not. That wheelchair represented his pride. His manhood. His body mended in that he could walk. But he was impotent. Something even his own doctor didn't know. He was quite incapable of being a complete husband.'

Baxter breathed, 'Good God!'

The woman said, 'Why on earth didn't he . . .'

'You who claim to "know" men.' There was friendly contempt in Pilter's tone. 'The one thing that *made* him a man. The wheelchair was his "hide". His excuse. To the world it was his reason for being incomplete. It stopped snide remarks. It gave him a measure of dignity.'

Baxter said, 'The poor bastard,' and there was little doubt but that he meant it.

And via some macabre working of mind and imaginings, a dead man seemed to join them in the room. A man long burned and buried. A man tormented by a passion and an ambition; a man who, like every other man on earth, had once been a tangled mass of contradictions. Loved and unloved; loving and hating; envied and admired; famed . . . and then unknown.

The Great Gordano. George Gordon.

Despite the warmth and comfort of the central heating a chill seemed to invade the room. A silence which made a mockery of time and seemed to last forever.

But just the one unseen ghost. Just the one; George Gordon . . . without his equally dead wife, Ruth.

Pilter eased the tension a little by lighting another cigarette.

Then the silence continued.

163

Very gently Pilter said, 'Why did you hate your sister?'

'I . . . didn't.' It was a very half-hearted denial.

'Not at first,' smiled Pilter. 'But eventually.'

'She had everything.' In the same toneless voice she corrected herself. 'She *seemed* to have everything. A husband who doted on her. That . . . and other things. She took it for granted. She took too much for granted.'

'She even tried to take *your* husband.'

Baxter protested, 'Look for God's sake . . .'

'I didn't know.' Baxter need not have been there; for what notice either of them took of him, Baxter need not have been there. She said, 'I didn't know . . . the other thing. It seemed unfair. Foul.'

'Tears,' mused Pilter gently. 'The only tears shed throughout the whole case.' He paused, then added, 'And another thing . . . you listen from behind closed doors.'

She nodded.

'Look what the hell are you two . . .'

'Tell him,' she said.

Pilter turned in his chair, faced Baxter and said, 'A murder, Mr Baxter. The murder of George Gordon. Your wife and I are the only two people on God's earth who know it. You'll be the third person, but because you know about the other thing – because your wife's told you about *that* – there'll never be a fourth.

'The day after the murder – the day after Gordon had been fed potassium cyanide – I called to see Mrs Gordon. Your wife was there at the time. She – er – broke down under questioning. She wept. She ran from the room, but she listened from behind the closed door. How do I know that? Well, we'll come to that later.'

Pilter drew on his cigarette then continued, 'Prior to that – prior to calling on Mrs Gordon – I'd had a chat with Hulda Deschin. I'd learned things. Things about stage magic. Her father – you know this of course – her father, like Gordon,

164

had once been a stage magician. Miss Deschin knew the tricks of the trade. Told me about them . . . about Gordon.

'Then, of course, Ruth Gordon. Ruth Gordon, your wife and Hulda Deschin were at the house when I arrived. Mrs Gordon couldn't decide. Suicide? Murder? First one, then the other. Undecided . . . and yet *not* undecided. I think the better word would be "fluctuating". Waiting for somebody else to say the word. The forbidden word "murder". I – er – I played an old police trick on her. An old conjurer's trick. I distracted her with some pointless arguments – suggestions – about Gordon's possible religion. Then I slipped in a suggestion, that Gordon might have palmed the condom packet, dropped the potassium cyanide into his own drink, then slipped the empty condom packet into your breast pocket.' Pilter's lips moved into a quick, sad smile and he ended, 'She fell.'

'Fell?' Baxter looked puzzled.

Pilter said, 'There wasn't a flicker of surprise when I mentioned the condom packet.'

'Oh!'

'No surprise,' said the woman softly. 'Even from behind the door I could tell that. I could hear. I was an audience. Like Mr Pilter, that was when I *knew*.'

'Good God!'

'Not,' said Pilter, 'the sort of – er – "container" *usually* used . . . except, of course, for condoms. Certainly not the sort of thing *women* carry around.'

'But you . . .' The woman smiled at her husband. Without rancour. Without even accusation. 'Just the sort of thing *you* might have.'

'Y'see,' explained Pilter, 'she'd once been Gordon's principal assistant. She could palm things, she'd learned the art well with The Great Gordano. Carry things, place things, hide things. Before hundreds of watching eyes . . . and without anybody seeing a thing. Compared with some of the things

165

she'd had to do carrying the packet, slipping the powder into the drink, then the packet into a man's outside breast pocket . . . like sucking toffee.'

'And you knew?' Baxter asked his wife the question.

'I guessed,' she said. 'After listening from behind the door . . . I was as good as sure. Later – when Mr Pilter had left – I tackled her. Yeah.' She nodded grimly. 'No proof. That was her big let-out. She was right, too.'

'She actually confessed?' said Pilter.

'If you call gloating a confession. She was a little like her own husband . . . cool. The right word. You could have taped that conversation. Word for word, it meant nothing. It was what she *didn't* say. It was a confession, all right.'

Pilter leaned forward, squashed his cigarette into the ashtray and murmured, 'So . . . *you* killed *her*.'

If it was meant as a question nobody answered. If it was meant as a statement of fact, nobody confirmed or denied it.

'Didn't you?' Pilter made it a gentle but blunt question. He raised his eyes to look at the woman's face without raising his head.

'Could be,' she fenced.

'Meaning of course . . .' Pilter relaxed back into his chair. 'Meaning to kill yourself at the same time.'

'Thank God she didn't,' said Baxter softly.

'If . . .' The woman chewed her lower lip, then said, '*If* I did?'

'She's dead,' said Pilter. 'The verdict was "Death by Misadventure".'

'Was, but shouldn't have been.'

Almost wearily, Pilter said, 'You wore a safety-belt. Your sister didn't. Your sister was driving. Her own car, a Mini. A fast car which she drove at speed. Your thumbprint. *Your* thumbprint . . . the same print from the face of your own wrist-watch. At a point on the steering wheel of the Mini. A point which would be at eleven o'clock, with the front wheels of the car pointing forward. Eleven o'clock, on the rim of the steering-wheel . . . and your *right* thumbprint.'

She breathed, 'Oh!'

'Where you grabbed the steering-wheel and spun the car off the road.'

'I – I intended us both to die,' she said softly.

'Of course.' Pilter nodded his understanding.

'It was – it was . . .'

'It was,' interrupted Pilter, 'a matter of killing two birds with one stone . . . a strangely appropriate expression. Your sister – much like her husband – without the capacity to love . . . to *truly* love. You disliked her. She humiliated you. Then she murdered her husband and deliberately planted the only real evidence on *your* husband. Love. Love and hatred . . . neighbouring emotions. You were – still are – capable of both.' He grinned. Almost chuckled. It was a spontaneous brightening of the face, almost child-like in its cheerful disregard of propriety. He said, 'Y'know . . . this has been quite an evening. The opera. Good company. A friendly chat. No coppers around to ask awkward questions. And everything just right.'

But it wasn't . . . not *just* right.

GEORGE GORDON

Bickering. The never-ending bickering. The bickering and the make-believe. Everlasting and (or so it seemed) since time began.

The agency 'worked'. Damn it to hell, couldn't they see that? The only yardstick worth a toss . . . that a thing 'worked'. The only illusion worth a damn had been one that 'worked'. As with everything. If a thing 'worked', that was enough; don't screw the thing to hell and beyond trying out improvements because, if the improvements buggered the thing up, they weren't improvements. A thing 'worked' or a thing didn't 'work'. That was the dividing line. Simple. Clear-cut. No arsing around with theories which might . . . or might not. A thing 'worked', it 'worked' . . . period.

Neil. As bad as the rest. Never bloody-well satisfied. Creaming good milk like crazy; offering blue muck as a by-product of a damn good agency. Not even having the gump-tion to realise that, if he hadn't played spin-ball, he'd have been a fifty-fifty partner by this time. Trust a man, then bring him in. But first make sure he's trustworthy. And if he turns out to be sour, forget it. Leave him to mess his own nest. Like Neil . . . not even having the sense to realise that, one day, some concert secretary would ring up, ask for something the agency wasn't supposed to handle, and let the cat fly out of the bag. On that day Neil was a non-runner. Out. Kaput. A man on a strict hire-and-fire basis. And kept on because

168

*of his wife. Because of Celia. Because to feed Neil to the dogs
would mean giving Celia even more misery.*

*Celia . . . why in hell's name did she soak up all this
bastardy from her husband? Why? Love? Well, maybe. He
(Gordon) wouldn't know. He wasn't the world's expert on
these things. Love – dime-novel love – was strictly for the
yum-yums of the earth. The dreamers. The women – yeah,
maybe the men – who lived life in their own personalised
kindergarten. The Peter-Pan-and-Wendy types. And they got
hurt. Sure they got hurt – what else? And all that smart-arse-
would-be-tough-girl talk of Celia's didn't hide a damn thing.
Inside that hard shell she was a mass of broken pieces; every
day of her miserable life she bled a little more.*

*So why add to the agony? Why tear the wings from an
already-damaged butterfly?*

And . . . talking about butterflies.

*Why, for Christ's sake, couldn't that candy-floss yuck
Dearden get it into his feminine little skull that he was here
to take pictures. That's all. Something not too far removed
from a Box Brownie job. Something simple and glossy. Something to turn out by the hundred for distribution to the
customers; to be pinned to a notice-board: to be glanced at
in passing. Not a would-be-work-of-art to be drooled over
and 'understood'. Nothing like that. Like the label on a bottle
. . . as simple and as uncomplicated as that. So why the hell
couldn't he take the money and do as he was damn-well
told?*

*Okay – maybe he was being pushed from behind by
Hector . . . by his bedmate.*

*The pansies of the showbiz crowd. Too many of them. A
load of old roots about 'deeper feelings'. Crap! Bullshit! A
bloody photographer and a guitar-plucker. What else for
God's sake? A group – and never mind about all that smarmy
talk about 'a band' . . . the real bands wouldn't have been*

found dead churning out the garbage The Ectoplasm called 'music'. They wouldn't have been found dead!

And now Ruth.

No good. No go. The marriage had been wrong from the first. The two of them . . . too much alike. Mr and Mrs Identical. That's what they were. That's what they'd always been. Something missing. Something missing, even before that blasted fall from the stage. Both demanding top spot and neither willing to move over.

Yeah . . . well.

This was one way. One way to stop the bickering. One way to jump the queue. One way to kybosh all the years of make-believe as far as this blasted chair was concerned.

And – dammit – she couldn't even do what she'd been taught properly.

What the hell it was she'd palmed. What the hell it was she'd dropped into his drink. What the hell it was she'd slipped into Neil's pocket. Any street-corner con-merchant could have spotted it . . . that's how clumsy she'd been. After all the practice. After all the tricks he'd taught her. Clumsy. Bloody clumsy.

And what was it? Goodbye-drops . . . what else?

The hell with it.

It was one way out . . .

The Great Gordano made his exit with a flourish, which, fifteen years previously, he would have approved. The 'stage set' of his departure had the subdued luxury which over the years had become his hallmark; elegantly styled drapes, colour without gaudiness, an impression of wealth without brashness. He even had an audience.

He tipped the rum-and-pep down his throat, returned the glass to the side-table by his elbow, seemed about to say something, then flopped forward in his wheelchair and sprawled awkwardly on the thick-piled carpet . . . and the trick was complete.

He was quite dead.

His greatest trick . . . to leave a puzzle nobody could solve.